SUN BURN

written by
Arthur Vincent Campbell, IV

with
visual translation by
Maria Grzech

and
research and footnotes by
Henry Rawlinson

T. PLATE SHIFT PUBLISHING
Bangkok • New York

ISBN-13: 978-0615573861

"ONE DAY you wake up and it's still a dream,
So it takes a while, blinking, thinking,
Surrounded by things strange, though just seen.
Barely touch it and it touches back.
Look at how things speak with little hidden lips:
A language unknown.
Bits about us swirl in dance,
And we shimmy in this old cartoon.
   – a row of singing flowers, hips without bones,
We smile though we know what it is:
    an alien dream left here alone.
Out of the last understandable mind
We shall all be left,
Here, in the place, our home."

[unhearable sound of a spaceship zinging through the galaxy]

The Radical Pump Boy's
"Sonic Sonnet"

I knew him. And this is his story.
So far as I know, it is true. And I have done my best to capture his view
of the world and his philosophy of existence, his sense of space and time,
his unintentional sense of humour. If you read this elastic biography, it
will change your mind, as writing it has changed mine.

Just ask Little Bo Peep.

Arthur Vincent Campbell, IV
Edinburgh, March 2007

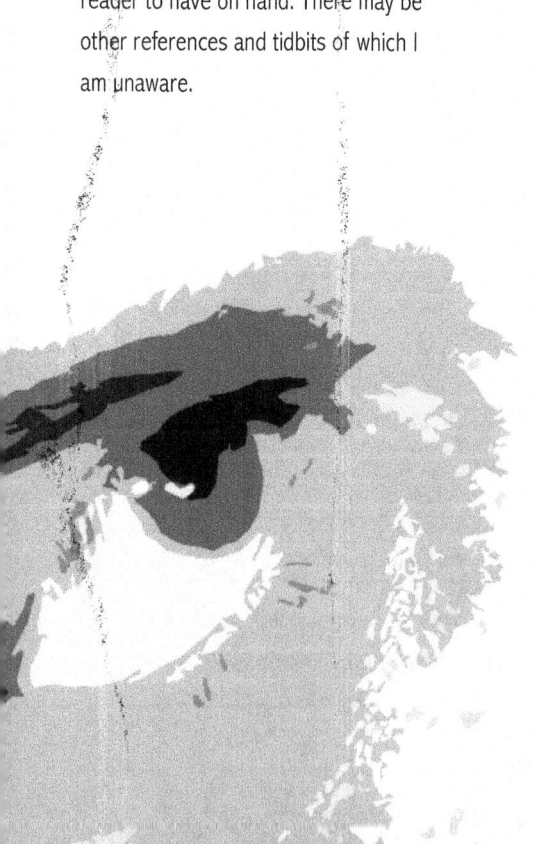

Notes to Book One

*Compiled by H. D. Rawlinson in order to reduce
unrealistic demands placed upon the reader.*

The self-indulgent, unnecessary complexity
wielded by Campbell is what turned-off publishing
houses in the first place. In addition to the lack
of conventional plot and character development,
of course. The first draft was even more
self-consciously artistic. I have examined
a number of references in the work, and
I have noted certain bits of knowledge
that the author evidently presumes the
reader to have on hand. There may be
other references and tidbits of which I
am unaware.

CHAPTER 1

The East Coast of the United States.
Sometime soon.

There was no more gas to pump ...
Time to take a drive ...

◄ ▬ ▬ ▬ ▬ ▬ ▬ ▬ ▬ *yet another reason* ▬ ▬ ▬ ▬ ▬ ▬ ▬ ▬ ►

"At sixty miles an hour, I think it's dangerous."

The Radical Pump Boy, partly forced-fantasy passed, and part perturbed rumble: ice-cold beer, fuzzy girlfriend, and self-installed, electrically controlled mirror all suspended over a silent second: gliding over the rubble-fringed asphalt wrapped in a supportive thumping rhythm and pleasing humming tone ... or was It? Saxophone, telephone, no-one-at-home sort of tone, or just kind of drive ... jive ... to the bone.

He liked that.

"Yes, I do think that it is dangerous ... all of it."

No answer from the fuzzy girlfriend turning up the outdated chrome radio dials with bright fingers tipped as dipped in suddenly frozen liquid red, and draped in dangling, seemingly inseparable, smoke. Was he the same person in the mirror? Who was looking at whom? And where did all those rocks come from? Where had the vegetation gone, and when? Why did everything he thought about end in a question mark?

That was the Rad world: he'd made it himself, or discovered it. Or at least questioned it.

All the while, the enemy was firing rockets at him. They were disguised as white dashes whizzing by on the centre of the road, an otherwise lonesome strip of wet black tar.

"Crowds like these of menacing rocks could be waiting for anyone ... and perhaps should be turned into gravel by large

3

[1] TRPB 104.248.7104
This is the actual highest
statistical possibility; and it
has been carefully, although
not exactly neatly, calculated
in Campbell's notes.

crushing machines: ideally the machines would be making a great deal of noise and providing dangerous jobs for industrious types struggling to pay for pink houses and olive dogs ... even a new stereo or a propane-propelled grill, preferably red, with a lot of smoke coming out of it. That's all that it's about."

"Shut up and watch what you're doing," burst out of the smoke.

Silence followed.

Thoughts were being reorganized: had he lost his job? Was he still pumping gas? Or was he still working for the Water Authority? Had he sold the company that repaired musical instruments? Had that been profitable? Why had the new girl shown up dripping wet on a clear day? Why did so many things make such little sense? Why were people always either giving orders or asking questions?

Perhaps it was simply thinking about things that made them so strange.

"I had all these broken instruments, but minor moods in cash flow and worker adagio, Gregorian bankers, and dripping wet Beautiful Largo Lips for a receptionist, who never talked right because she had a treble clef. Well, either that or ... maybe it was something that started in the ice age."

The Pump Boy looked at Fuzzy for a reaction. Nothing.

He tried again: "I hear bells. . .ancient church bells. A bell ringer, you know, with seven bells, ringing triples, can produce five thousand and forty changes." [1]

"What does that have to do with repairing anything?"

"Well, nothing, I suppose. It's just what they can do. It's a real talent."

"Talent?" she said, "Some guy spending his life ringing bells in the middle ages?"

"Well, not really the middle ages," Rad tried, "It was later than that. Time is such an odd thing once it's used up"

"So how much has been used up?"

Rad wanted to get off the subject. "All of it," he said, "at least so far."

Maybe he hadn't sold the company after all.

"We should have some gas by tomorrow, and I can go back to pumping. It's exciting when the car window opens: every car has a different person inside."

"You just missed your turn."

"Sorry. Forgot. I'll try again."

There appeared to be a tremendous surge of power as Rad stabbed at the gas pedal,

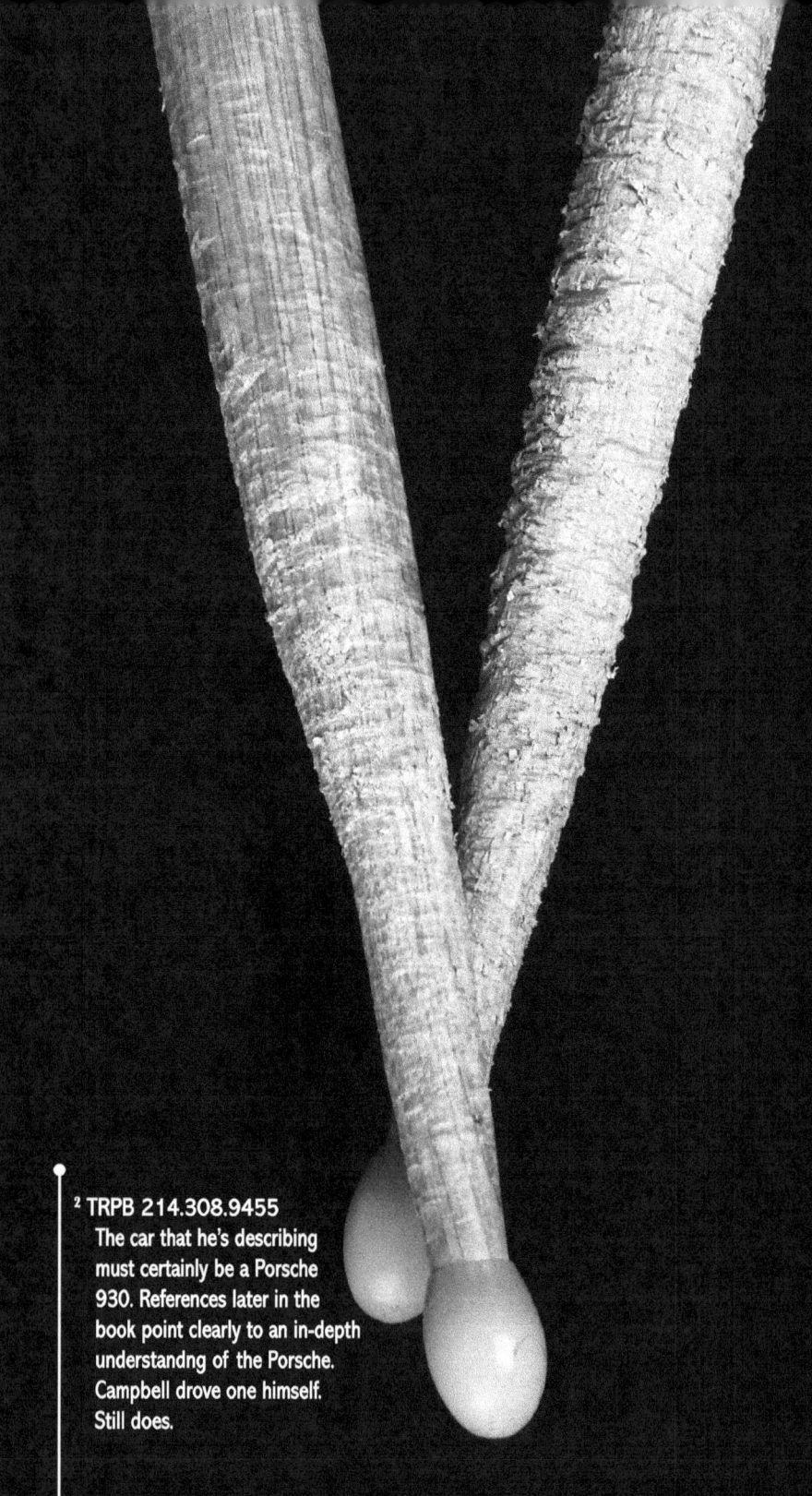

² TRPB 214.308.9455
The car that he's describing
must certainly be a Porsche
930. References later in the
book point clearly to an in-depth
understandng of the Porsche.
Campbell drove one himself.
Still does.

the boost being augmented by sound effects of The Pump Boy's own design: "I love German engines, especially turbo charged, air-cooled engines that run at suicidally high RPM levels!" [2]

"This is a Rambler. You been spendin' too much time with that mechanic."

"Oh ... well ... I see. This is a Rambler. Well, they look good in green, don't they?"

"Jesus! Turn here, would ya!"

A pack of cigarettes on the dash was wrapped in cellophane, adorned with a yellow animal. Tobacco eyes were peeking out, maybe plotting an escape, maybe wearing make-up and eyebrows of light blue ink.

And there she was: rummaging around in that criminal pocketbook made of endangered Naugahyde and fastening it with that deceptive ping. What was she doing in there? All that rustling and jumbling, fingers searching for some lost item in that pouch of chaotic possessions.

She had it: a cigarette lighter.

He glanced at the dashboard. They were still there ... now benign and suspecting nothing, almost inanimate in appearance, bathing in the sun and warm heat of the dash as if it were some sort of resort for half-empty cigarette packs.

Life seemed cruel and careless.

He couldn't bear to watch. "You know, if I sold the business, I'd have more time to work at the garage ... or maybe rearrange furniture. Of course, there is an old accordion that I'd want to retain ... or have I? Maybe it's not a part of the deal. And I'd also like to keep one of the drums, preferably the black ones with the rectangular silver sparkles ... and one of those scratch vests that you play with spoons. They're cool: something between mediaeval armour and a man from space."

From a cloud of smoke, and over the final, fading sounds of a dying cigarette on his funeral pyre: "What's with the drum? I don't get it. This beer's kinda warm."

So The Pump Boy kept his attention on the road, more or less, dodging the missiles and watching frightened faces whiz by like colour-coded televisions running wild and unplugged.

"I like ... I think ... I'd like to have a drum."

"Is it better than a business?"

"Yes, I ... believe that it is a lot smaller, and more fun to play."

She shook her head in the smoke cloud.

"You're wonderful," The Pump Boy sniffed, "but I think it would be better if we spoke different languages. Then it would be more like music ... or engine noises ... or ... like all these question marks."

Fuzzy looked at Rad and then faded away, shaking her head in the smoke, flashing wet red nails like planets circling a fidget of a sun.

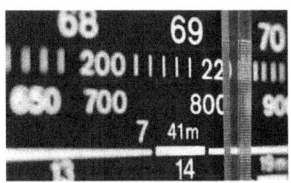

CHAPTER 2

Fuzzy was buying fingernails, and Business was thawing around mahogany veneer.

At the bank.

Constant chatter was chewing on Radical Pump's ear.

Not sure whether he was talking or listening, he squinted at Hammering Jim, King of the Lawyers, who was rat-a-tat-tatting with looks of ballooning apprehension and increasing colouration. A banker and someone else were sitting across the veneer plain from Jim. It was interesting. But damn that chewing on his ear.

He wondered how long it would take before the chewing reached his brain, and when it did, what it would find there. He had always conjectured that looking into the brain would be like looking into a mirror, only that the glass wouldn't be hard and all the words wouldn't be backwards ... or would they? You'd be able to reach out and touch everything even though it wouldn't really be there.

"Jim, I like it when you say smoke and mirrors," Rad ventured.

But the compliment first seemed to upset the Lawyer King.

People get upset over things that d on't even make any sense.

Radical Pump was still envisioning his own brain, and brain time, now with diaphanous wisps of smoke seeping out and sliding down the mirror. He was almost afraid to touch it.

"Let's go to the garage, Jim."

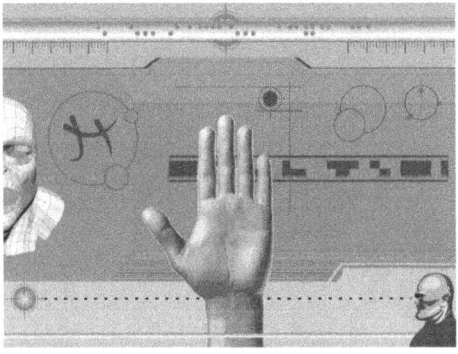

CHAPTER 3

THE GARAGE

Moe was skittering around under a chocolate-coloured car on a streamlined skateboard while interrogating an automatic transmission through an impotent cigar butt. This was what the ATR crowd got into. Automatic Transmission Repairmen, that is. They talked to themselves or they talked to things that couldn't possibly answer back. Sometimes both.

The jerking Radical Pump Boy interrupted to ask Moe's boots about the gas situation.

The boots wobbled back and forth while the cigar butt grunted irritably that there was still no gas. Radical fingered his necktie, trickling over it as if it were an oboe.

He noticed that it had been cut in half about two-thirds of the way down. Examining carefully the amputation, he concluded that it must have been executed by a very sharp pair of scissors ... or maybe not so sharp.

"I have to go, Moe. Hammering Jim is waiting in the car. I think he's talking to the radio."

"That's okay with me, Rad."

Radical noted that the boots weren't moving back and forth any more and figured that there wasn't any more conversation in there anyway.

OBJECTS IN MIRROR ARE CLOSER THAN THEY APPEAR

[3] TRPB 987.456.0985
Traditional Mercedes-Benz
arrangement.

CHAPTER 4

THE ROAD

The unusually bright sun was a boiling burning droplet on the hood of Jim's highly polished sedan. The hot pool of light interfered with the car's front sighting apparatus.

These things worried Radical Pump.

Hammering Jim's increasingly gesticulated conversation was thumping and tugging on the expensive-looking steering wheel. Jim totally ignored the continual dashing volley of missiles whizzing past.

Radical wondered what Hammering Jim could possibly be going on about. He also wondered what would happen if the car were to drift into the path of the missiles.

"Does this car have electrically adjustable mirrors, Jim?"

"Huh?... Of course. Well, mine is manual, but the one for your side is right here," thumping on the centre console. [3] "Why?"

"I want to use it."

"Help yourself. Listen, another thing that worries me about Moe is his apparent complete lack of ability to get anything ... even the most simple task ... completed. He ... how long has that car been in there for the transmission work? That's the same car that was there last month. And the month before that. How can all that inventory disappear against work orders that haven't been fulfilled ..."

Blah, blah, blah.

Going, going, going on ...

But Radical had the mirror.

Radical could clearly see the stream of missiles vanishing down the highway behind the car, miraculously slicing through traffic without incident.

[4] TRPB 004.115.6208
Legal term: when a judgment overrides the verdict. I think it's used here mainly for the sound, but only because I haven't figured it out yet.

[5] TRPB 165.222.1298
A beautiful perpetual canon, attributed to Wm. Byrd and containing hidden octaves, crafted with great ingenuity. It's written in the Mixolydian Mode and is famous to the esoterics.

[6] TRPB 108.251.6624
State law permitting the state to exercise jurisdiction over an out-of-state defendant. Rad gets around a bit.

[7] TRPB 100.428.5716
Statue of liberty.
Why was he there?
Immigrant?

dEstINAtIoN

"Say Jim, do you see anything unusual in this mirror here?"

Jim suspended the dialogue and glanced at the mirror.

"No. But damn if you haven't gotten it all outta whack! I'm seeing telephone poles where I should be seeing cars!"

Jim groped for the control, orchestrating several whirs and clicks. He seemed satisfied with the adjustment.

Radical squinted over the sun-pocked dark hood, peering through the car's front sight. Jim was babbling on the left and juggling a telephone, a black plastic telephone that was beeping a lot but not saying anything. The beeping sounds were electronic and didn't imitate the sound of any known musical instrument. Jim was questioning the phone about a non *obstante veredicto*,[4] which didn't represent any known musical term and probably

wasn't related to the famous canon, *Non nobis Domine*.[5]

Radical tried to picture the long arm statute [6] that Jim was discussing: the stone creaked and groaned when the statute walked. Its massive arm, typically held aloft, would occasionally drop heavily on small suburban houses, scattering patio furniture, plastic toys, and eliciting a chorus of barking dogs. There was no stopping such a statute. It had been carved from sick rocks. There was no machine big enough to crush it. Why was it evil? Was it evil? Was it related to the big green woman with the flaming hand?

A flaming hand and a head emitting daggers.[7] He'd been there before, but when? There had been a job interview that had not gone well because his necktie had been cut in half.
Or ... had it gone well?

8 TRPB 845.205.1273
Weird 1983 movie about an alien
spacecraft that lands on Earth.
The aliens are in search of
chemicals given off during human
sex. An unsightly but oddly gripping
subculture piece. Unusual.

9 TRPB 003.200.1361
Phone number was for
"Little Bo Peep – *helps make
up minds.*"

Waitress on an ordinary limb.
Hugging him.

Ah, the next morning was arriving as the dream got noisy: almost empty yellow sneakers chasing an empty egg carton and chirping on a glass floor. Almost awake now.

The black hole over which the frail curtain had been drawn was now emitting a frightening glow. An impending, radioactive announcement of inevitable day.

What was it going to be like out there? Excruciating mysteriousness, just like every other day – at least so far. What was it like now?

There was a fresh collection of matchbooks on the shimmering night stand: one was red with a bird in a box and another with a broom; one said *Change my mind* and the other *Not too soon.*

Rad studied the designs while maintaining a paranoid vigil over the shimmering and ever-increasing hazy glow. It reminded him of a movie title that he had seen somewhere:

Liquid Sky.[8] But research had indicated that the movie itself had nothing to do with the sky at all. Something had been scribbled in the *Change my mind* matchbook.[9] Looked like Rad-writing all right. Have to give her a call someday.

Rad glanced at the TV. Someone had taped a photocopy of a test pattern to the screen.

May as well get up and at it.

The antique chrome cold-water faucet turned with a characteristically rusty eek, eek, eek sound of a cartoon. It limply dribbled some titanium-coloured fluid, reminding the continuously awakening Pump Boy that it was his turn to work at the Water Authority.

The fluid stopped, and there was nothing but a damp, dark green path to the drain, and descending gurgitations, deep into

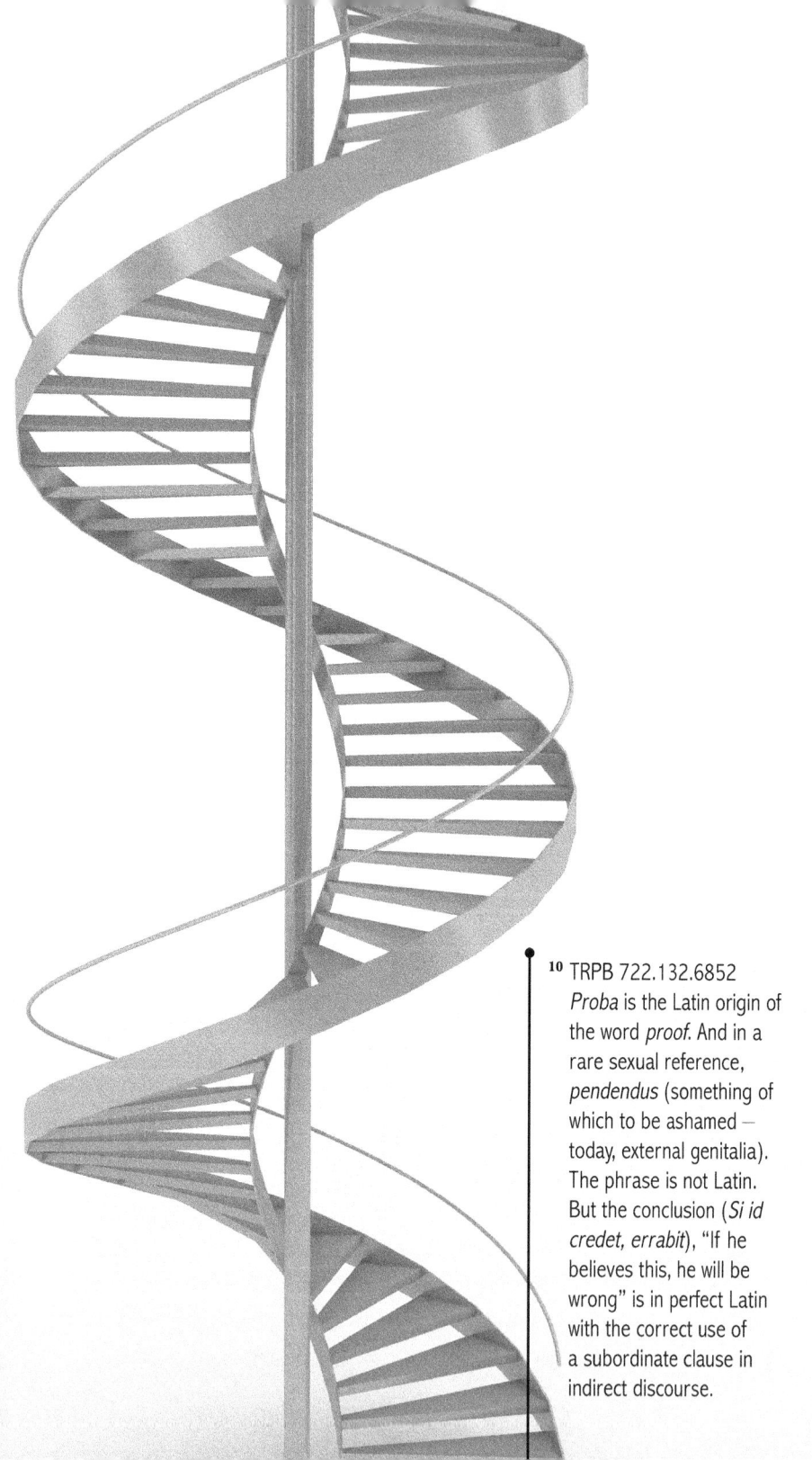

¹⁰ TRPB 722.132.6852
Proba is the Latin origin of the word *proof.* And in a rare sexual reference, *pendendus* (something of which to be ashamed — today, external genitalia). The phrase is not Latin. But the conclusion (*Si id credet, errabit*), "If he believes this, he will be wrong" is in perfect Latin with the correct use of a subordinate clause in indirect discourse.

somewhere beyond.

Rad looked down the drain. There was nothing there.

Eek, eek, eek on the hot side: Nothing there either.

"No water. Okay. So where's my uniform?"

Radical Pump rummaged pointillistically through a heap of periodicals and personal effects … parts of blue and yellow plastic toys, a convincingly golden lipstick tube with a bright red recluse, a green uniform, a blue one, an expensive Italian suit made of stainless steel, and … here: a grey jumper with the official badge of the Known Water Authority.

Good. Of course, he still had to find the shoes.

But was he late? Hard to say. Someone had taped a test pattern over the still-breathing, always incongruent, alarm clock.

"Life is just a test, they say," the Pump Boy assured himself, "and all this is proof of that. As the Romans used to say *"Proba de doba doba. Endus pendentus. Si id credet, errabit."* [10]

It was now increasingly and frighteningly bright and noisy outside. Everywhere was overwhelming light and noise: slurping from hissing blocks of chrome-enhanced colour blocks, riveting from machine frenzy, and always, filmed under streetlights, dying. Forgotten lullabies. Car keys jingling. Songs singing themselves. Rad was talking to himself again, wasn't he?

"We have made our machines bigger than we are," he noted. "They even eat more than we do."

Well. Work to do.

After carefully and artfully cleaning all the glass to a calibrated squeakiness, Radical Pump plopped into the Rambler, took a deep, restorative, and comfortable breath of funky old car smell, and ignited the trusty power plant from yesteryear.

No explosion.

Great! The day was off to a good start: no one had wired a large explosive device in parallel with the ignition circuits. Suspects could have been plentiful: that guy who wanted his trombone back had been acting pretty intense about it for the past three months. What if he had a friend or a brother in the explosives business? What if he had taken a Boy Scout course in demolition?

Rad looked at his eyebrows in the rearview mirror, made a hand signal, paused, and pulled away from the curb while shrugging his shoulders: "Well, as they say: The best laid plans of mice and men often take place on the moon."

Radical scanned the dash for a pack of cigarettes: nothing. All alone.

[11] TRPB 080.055.9595
This is probably pointing
to Tchaikovsky's opus 30,
quartet No. 3 in E-flat
minor (strings). Why?
I don't know yet.

What was she doing today?

She had some kind of job that she talked about all the time. But what? Or ... so what?

Radical was picturing the architectural plan view of the city, the road map in his mind (a good way to get around). He found the part with the large grey doors of the Known Water Authority. Oh yes. He was thinking about the blue kinescopic glow that infected his staff, and obviously drew some kind of energy from their depreciating minds.

Thousands of characters concocted from binary data patterns performed distracting dances while the minds of the masses were tapped for alpha-kinetic energies. Or something like that. What would happen when all the kinescopes were replaced with flat screen terminals?

He paused again, thinking that he could be technically wrong. Let's see, alpha waves equal to half the product of their mass and the square of their velocity ... but for brain waves? No matter. He was the manager and didn't have to squint at monitors, as they are oddly named *(well, not very often, anyway)*.

Stabbing at the gas pedal and enunciating the appropriate sound effects, Rad overtook a large, smoking Lincoln and sailed effortlessly down the motorway.

He was thinking about his girl friend. He was thinking about their last conversation: the last one that he could remember, anyway.

"How about some music?" He had asked.

"No way, I don't wanna hear any more of that what's-his-name-osky's quartets number 3 in C-flat major stuff."

Long pause.

"It can't be in C-flat," he corrected.

"What? It doesn't matter. It's just an expression."

"Well, if it's just an expression, you may as well change it to E-flat. I mean, it just doesn't make sense otherwise. Osky doesn't do C-flat. So say E-flat minor — which would make more sense." [11]

She had attempted to stare down the Pump Boy, but that doesn't work very well unless someone is looking at you ... or giving a damn.

"Make more sense?" the Fuzzy Head replied in peripheral vision, "To you, E-flat makes more sense and C-flat doesn't? What the hell kind of world is that?"

"Hmmm. The western musical world," Rad said, "And, then again, I suppose you're right. It's a very small place, that. So ... uh ... I have *Sounds of the Humpback Whale* ... "

She hadn't wanted to hear that either.

CHAPTER 6

The dead ones are the efficient ones.
Insects leave blinding hum in the air
Vultures follow ... a feast is born.
This green-fly delight.
Ta-tum, ta-tum.
Where are we from?
Where are we from?

The grey doors were locked.

Broken glue-on fingernails glittered the sidewalks with unmistakable signs of a struggle. Otherwise quiet, supervised only by a fire escape ladder, which descended from nowhere, hovering just over the street. Some trash, car parts, other stuff more difficult to identify. Just the usual everywhere stuff.

The cold, retread tyre ... was dead.

A spiraling pirouette of leaves and litter approached, supported by a choking gust of street breeze. It lost its balance over the retread; the breeze died, and collapsed: another one dead.

"Another with the broom," Radical thought, momentarily picturing the cryptic matchbook cover before replacing the image with that of a newspaper headline that he had suddenly recalled:

EX-HARD-HAT RETIRES ...
SAYS HE PREFERS RETREADS ...
or something like that.

Cha-chink!

Clad in the iridescent foil of a space blanket with blue piping, Officer KillFlash turned the corner and clicked his heat-seeking revolver at the Radical Pump Boy:

"Closed today ! What are you up to? Where did those fingernails come from? Why don't your shoes match ... and ... what's wrong with your tie ?"

Date. Yesterday 19 ✔

M 55179 - 345

Address (beats me)

		Account Forward	
Reg. No.	Clerk		
1	trombome alone		
2			
3	clean sticky valves		
4			
5	and add squeak-free oil		
6			
7			
8	price just parts		
9	and toil		
10			
11			
12			
13			
14			
15			

Your Account Stated to Date—If Error Is Fo

"I'm supposed to work here today," Rad replied (with a characteristically ambiguous authority).

"You're the guy from the Private Sector?"

"Yes."

"The guy with the instrument store and the frozen food warehouse ?"

"Store, yes. But I don't remember anything about a warehouse. But as they say: A bird in the hand is better than a frozen fish."

"You mean burning bush?" KillFlash lowered his revolver.

"My brother-and-law's got a trombone in your shop. How's it coming?"

"It's not good ... needs some rest." Radical looked down at his own feet that peeked out from the oversized uniform, casually noting that the shoes certainly didn't match at all. "... But," he continued professionally, "if I can't fix it, nobody can."

"That bad, huh?" KillFlash said, returning the revolver to its holster.

"Maybe. It's hard to tell sometimes when it comes to trombones. It's usually in the valves."

"My Dad had an artificial valve. It never worked the way it was supposed to, really. He worried about it all the time." KillFlash was starting to shift his weight from side to side. "Listen, nobody's been around this place for weeks. Whad'ya say we walk down to Larry's for a beer. My mechanic's usually in there, so I can get an update on my transmission problems. You got any transmission problem in your private sector?"

"No, I don't. Sorry about your Dad's valves. Maybe he has a lot of them, I've seen up to six — no, seven — but you only have three. It will be OK with the trombone.[12] What colour is your brother-in-law's car?"

"Brown ... I think. It's been in for a while."

Rad rolled his eyes up slightly — the way people do when they are trying to remember something. He wasn't sure that the technique was working though.

But close.

Larry's Limited Slip

Inside.

There were a lot of girls at Larry's place who looked like Fuzzy. She might have even been one of them, or possibly several of them, or — and most likely, Rad hypothesized — all of them. The place was very dark: there wasn't a clearly identifiable source of whatever light there was; and wherever the light came from, most of it was spread around by the multi-layered blankets of blue cigarette smoke, just floating around in it or vice versa. It smelled of ATF and hypoid oil: clear olfactory evidence that the place was

[13] TRPB 845.205.1273
Technical description of the
"outdated lettering" font.

[14] TRPB 003.200.1361
A complicated word mix-up game.
Rad obviously doesn't know what a
mixologist is, but he does know
that an antiquarian usually deals
in old books, hence his reference
to shelves. Rad is thinking of an
ancient Greek musical mode, later
used in the mediaeval church and
corresponding to the current
major mode with a minor 7th.

the local haunt of Automatic Transmission Repairmen.

It didn't look like the kind of place where you'd find a good woodwind man capable of putting new pads on a saxophone. But maybe you'd find a guy who could locate a leak in a bagpipe by holding the instrument under water and squeezing it (Radical had seen this done in Scotland and had never gotten over the brutality of the act: the grunting red face of the Highlander strangling the antique musical instrument in a primitive watering trough while cursing, "You damn'd bloated haggis: I'll save a place for you in the blackest burning hell!" It was no way to talk to a musical instrument ... especially considering the paradoxical thermodynamic oxymoron serving as the base of the threat).

"How about a drink?" questioned the bartender, who was wearing a toque with the name LARRY written across the brow in outdated lettering.

Radical spoke up: "Cooper bold, all caps.13 How old is it?"

"We don't serve no vintage nothin' here, you know that ... um? You the guy that asked me about the soup last week, you work for Moe ... right ... uh ... Rad."

"Right."

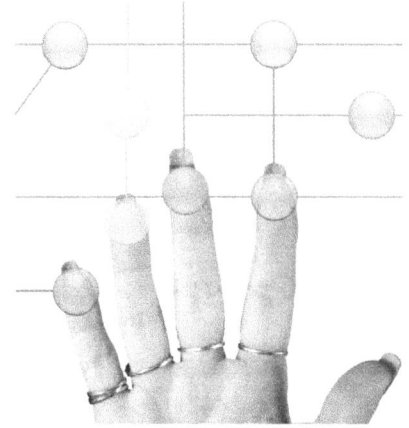

Larry looked halfway towards the officer, "This guy a friend of yours, Flash?"

Officer KillFlash was talking to one of the fuzzies and drawing a picture in the air as if telling a fish story. The fish wasn't very big, though.

Larry looked at Rad and shrugged: "I'm a mixicologist, not an antiquarian, Rad."

"I'll have one of those," said Rad, nodding at a brightly decorated bottle. "I have a grave respect for modus mixoldius."

Larry stared, rapping his fingers on the bar the way Hammering Jim was prone to do on tables.

"In other words, mixolydian, 14 " Rad offered, attempting to bridge the gap and starting to get quite thirsty as well, " I know you're not an antiquarian: even though you have lots of shelves in here. Ah ... one of those. Please."

Larry shook his head and pushed the drink in front of The Pump Boy.

[15] TRPB 070.112.9584
A limited slip differential is
a device in the automotive
drive line that splits the power
between the driving wheels.

CHAPTER 7

**Cardboard covered manholes.
Light bulbs strung like naked metal trinkets
tinkling like an insect swarm
thinking like warm jam
not in a jar but in a can.**

Geez ... late night thermal damage and mismanaged hair (that was standing straight up like a concrete block balanced luggage-rack-style on his head).

Alarm clock ringing. Across the room, the test pattern was exactly where it had been yesterday morning.

Radical groped for the water glass on the night stand. A book of matches was floating lifelessly in the titanium, slogan-side up.

It said: "Larry's Limited Slip ... *It's Differential*." [15]

Rad jerked a smile, "Neat pun."

He extracted the highly polished chrome matchbook, noting that, though clever, the slogan had been set in another outmoded and grotesque font: Souvenir! Perhaps even worse than Cooper Bold. But there was something interesting after all: inside the book, an inscription, now blurred and fractionally readable, portended *Early to bed and early to rise makes a potato head out of any guy.* The radical pump head bobbed up and down in oblique concurrence.

"Potato head," Rad noted, head still bobbing, "Potato head ... any guy."

Morning's vague plastic shutter fluttered for no apparent reason. Rad stuffed the matchbook into his remaining sock, which was yellow with black triangles superimposed over frail red circles. The socks were font-free.

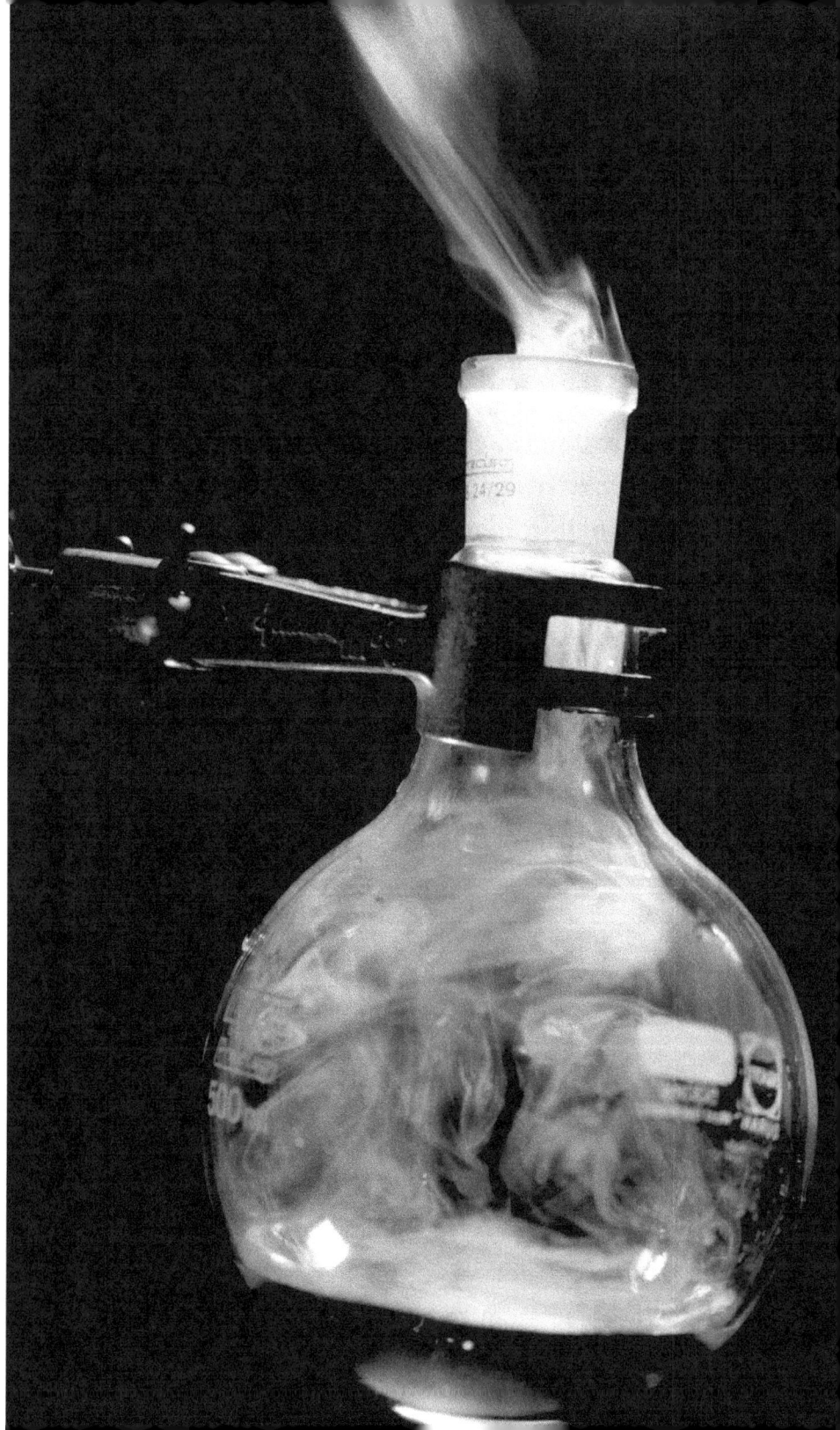

work, work
work again
long row to hoe
start all over again
work, work
but never for a jerk

Radical was delighted to see the big green tanker truck at the garage, disgorging its contents into the subterranean storage tanks that were monitored by underground sensors. There was some kind of relationship between the sensors and the ground water hydrocarbon count. Jim talked about it a good bit, but it all seemed rather trivial, since nobody wanted the tanks to leak in the first place. After all, the gas pumps themselves were so playful and benign. Moe had painted them to match his skateboard: a lot of yellow and black ... with day-glo green palm trees and other odd items in the tropical-motif genre.

The whole place reeked of high-octane gasoline.

It was an exciting smell.

Inside the garage, Moe was skittering around under a smallish sports car. Great clouds of cigar smoke rose from the swollen wheel wells ...

"So this guy wants a titanium spool in place of a differential. That will give him a full lock. And I guess we'll have to shaft it with titanium rear axles too, right. Then we'll start playing with the ratios. Then we'll have to work on the linkage. Even with the new-cone synchronizers, these things are still a hassle to shift."

Rad looked at the car. It reminded him of a large female lion hunkered down, paws stretched out ... ready to pounce on something very unlucky. The car only had two seats, which seemed like a good idea. But there wasn't any front sight at all. The front end just dropped away as if to keep its nose on the tarmac — sniffing for prey.

What else? Oh, there was a large brown sedan in the neighboring bay. Rad looked it over: probably wasn't an ounce of titanium in it. But it had a real neat front sight, although the sight wasn't as accurate looking as Hammering Jim's.

"Moe, this car doesn't have an automatic transmission. I've never seen this car before. It looks kinda like yours."

Rad looked back at the smoking sports car:

"Well sure, Rad. This sort of machinery doesn't exactly drop like fruit from a tree, ya know."

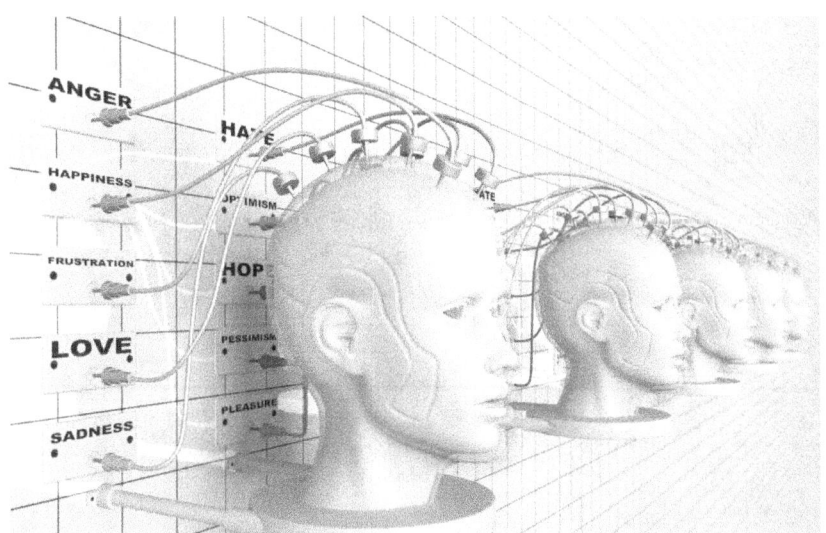

"Oh, I see. Well, I'm going out to talk to the gas truck man."

Radical was picturing a tree with cars dangling from it, suspended by strings — preferably yellow strings — and silver cars ... and a dark blue sky with a sliver of the moon still visible ... and Venus too (even though Saturn was his favourite). I suppose you could tune the strings and play a funky melody. That would be fun. Rad had never seen such a tree. Nor had he ever seen a fruit tree.

The gas tanker was interesting: it had lots of valves and tremendous lengths of articulated pipe. With these, it was possible to fill several underground tanks at once — well, that is, if an experienced operator were conducting the exercise. The best part was the air-brushed artwork that covered almost every square metre of the tanker. There were all sorts of names, symbols, and playful, refreshingly creative logos in bright colours. Layers upon layers of them. Everywhere.

"Neat paint job," Radical gawked.

"Look it, where I park this thing, it's a bad neighborhood. We get that stuff all over the place. There's nothin' I can do about it."

Rad wasn't even listening to the seemingly contradictory commentary.

"Do you know this guy ... SLAM MAN (be dam')?"

"Hey kid, what you see is what I know. That's it."

The Radical Pump Boy wondered about the visible image of knowledge. Perhaps it wasn't transparent ... like air, or like the other side of the mirror where the brain

16 TRPB 560.056.1111
I'm not sure what the author is after here. But Satie was a turn-of-the-century French composer known for atonal and polytonal compositions with bizarre names.

17 TRPB 043.564.7720
Music scholars: PIT are Tchaikovsky's initials, and Désirée Artôt was a successful opera singer to whom Tchaikovsky was attracted but failed to marry. He later married unsuccessfully at age 37 .

18 TRPB 032.987.1654
This seems to be another reference to the movie *Liquid Sky*, q.v.

hung out. Maybe this was what it actually looked like: spray-painted colours on a tremendous expanse of truck ... sort of a portable, functional Sistine Chapel. Or maybe it was all atonal – like Erik Satie in colour. [16]

Yes, some of the functional aspects had been sacrificed: the side window of the cab had been painted over with a stylized leopard paw and some Art Nouveau-influenced initials "P.I.T." (Rad wondered whether this might have something to do with Tchaikovsky, and whether perhaps the paw represented Désiree Artôt).[17] All that aside, the painted window seemed to violate general safety standards. Perhaps it had been done to block alien broadcasts from the right-side mirror. Rad checked for messages, but found nothing on the mirror.

Rad had never actually heard any alien broadcasts, but he had seen them. You could always spot an alien message by the way it didn't read backwards in a mirror ... or, at least, none that Rad had seen read backwards.

Aliens had different ways, after all, and even ate strange things: like cardboard ... or fruit that was red. Some of them came here for pheromones, which are thoughts and instructions that float through the air. [18] Of course, most of them drank too much, just like everybody else. And they didn't have doghouses. Plus they never played around with spheres; there were, come to think of it, no alien ball games at all. But ball games were everywhere on Earth. Maybe because the Earth was a sphere. Maybe that was the origin of all those games. Maybe that's why people say "round and round she goes, and where she stops, nobody knows?"

Aliens played with mirrors because that's where they came from.

Come to think of it, Rad couldn't recall ever having been anywhere that had as many mirrors as Larry's Limited Slip. It was like being inside a giant robot's brain, where everybody was a thought or an idea ... just standing around killing time like stunned brain cells, while the robot goofed off, or set fire to long-arm statutes.

CHAPTER 9

Sun strings around grey lumps of cloud.
Diesel smoke strokes the silver lining.

A pair of white-hot vanishing point light splinters and click clack, click clack. The Radical Pump Boy and ATR Moe were watching the railroad track (and watching, too, the big blue engine's smoke).

"Ya see, Rad, an automatic transmission can have a clutch. In fact, the best transmission, bar none, has two clutches so that you never break the power flow ... and it's automatic."

Two clutches? Power flow? The words were interesting. But the Boy couldn't imagine the mechanics ... even given his liberal latitude when it came to the visual translation of the intangible, which was then fighting to focus on a vague image of two complicated mechanical devices desperately holding on to each other while being swept away in the turbulent white waters of an unstoppable flow of power.

"That little red car ... come in Tuesday: it has a vacuum-operated clutch fired by a microswitch in the gear change lever. Plus it has a three-speed torque converter."

"Why would anybody name a day Tuesday, Moe? Especially over and over again?"

"I don't know about nothin' like that, Rad. I guess the Romans did it."

"No," Rad solemnized, while finishing the last crease in a crude paper airplane, "You're thinking of February."

[pause]

"Moe, what exactly does a torque converter look like?"

"Ah ... well, sort of like a big doughnut."

"Oh."

Rad conducted a brief but disappointing test flight.

Moe flipped a long arch of cigarette over the airplane wreckage. "Let's go back to town, Rad."

"Sure, Moe."

Thinking: Moe, probably the best-dressed automatic transmission repairman in the world, drove a car with a manual gear

change ... on the floor no less ... actually attached to it in fact. Moe seemed to fool around with the shift lever a lot while driving, as if it took some

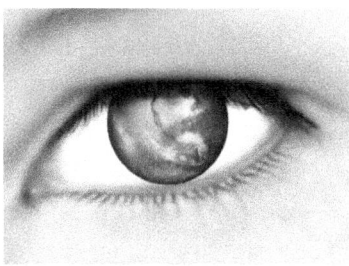

secret formula of movements and engine noises just to locate first gear. And then jump. Then Moe would do the combination thing again for second. And then jump again. All accompanied by a continuous pumping of the clutch leg and the leaping of the car.

Gas pedal leg. Clutch leg. Gear shift arm. Steering hand.

Rearview mirror.

"Moe, cars are a lot like robots, aren't they? But they use people for brains."

"I don't know, Rad. Depends on the car."

RPB looked around Moe's car: low, wide ... hunkered down ... no front sight at all. Like everything of Moe's, it had a skateboard-kind-of look. It was even flipped up at the back. It was obviously very purposeful, but what was its purpose? It was, he had it:

to be unyieldingly purposeful.

As always, the ride back to town was interesting (and just a little bit scary). Moe was intensely orchestrating all the levers,

pedals, and controls with phenomenological delight while he straightened out the otherwise twisted little road.

Since there was a picture window two inches from the Pump Boy, he watched his side of the exterior world unwind.

They passed a power station with nobody home. But there was a lot of industrial deco stuff that looked very complicated. It reminded Rad of a giant, industrial-strength xylophone caught in an alley full of overpopulated metallic clotheslines ... or something like that.

Then they passed a large herd of mustard-coloured bulldozers that was grazing on a vast pasture of raw Earth. Shepherds with plastic helmets were waving at the bulldozers.

Rad waved at the shepherds.

"Look, Moe: Bulldozers grazing."

There was a long pause – filled mainly with driving noises. Rad caught himself thinking about the instrument repair shop ... at least, that's what he thought he was thinking about. He was imagining a conversation with Largo Lips, the new girl, which, in reality, would be impossible.

"You know Largo Lips, Moe?"

"Sure, the lady with the Citroën SM.

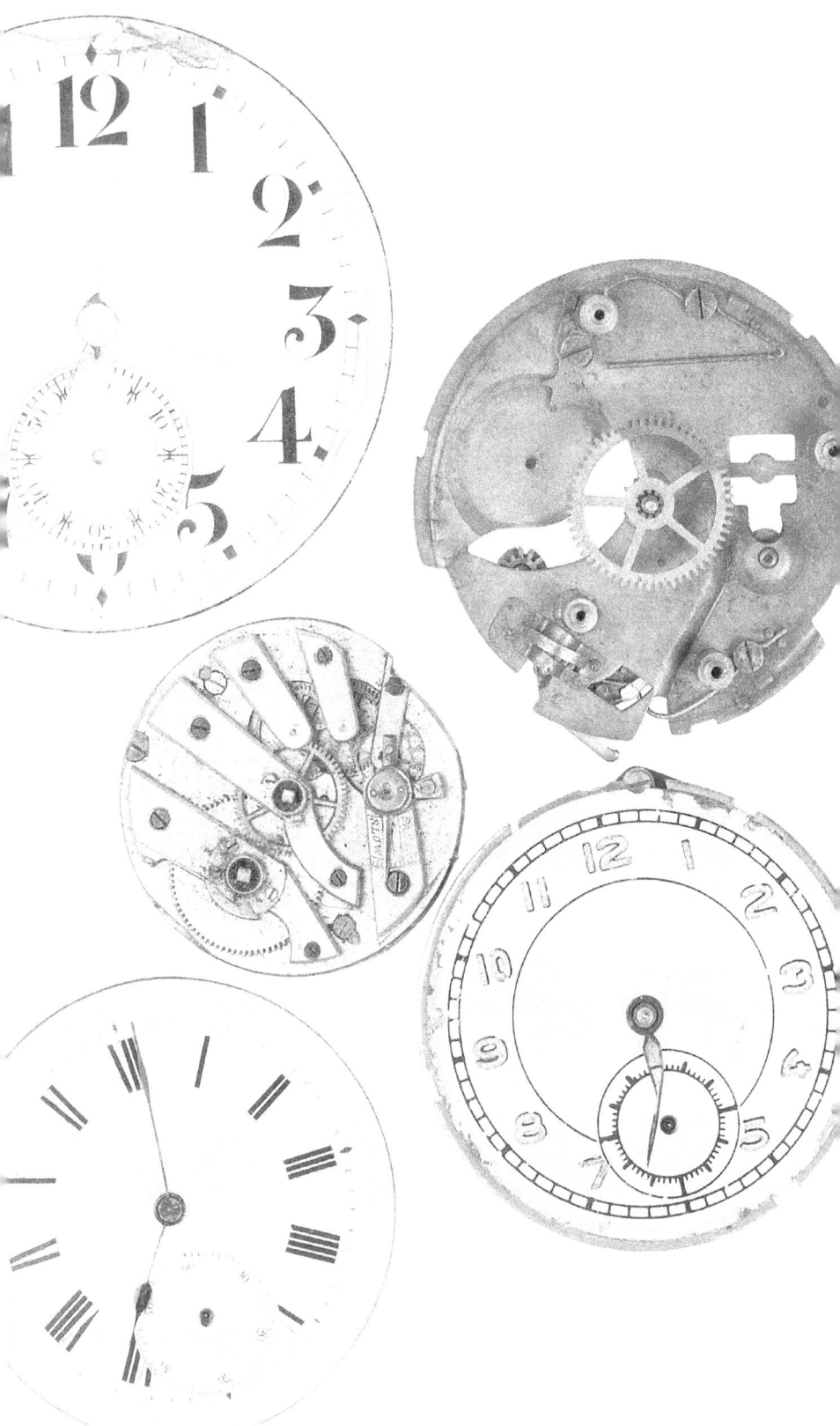

Nice car. Very French."

"She's interesting, don't you think? "

"Everything is interesting to you, Rad. I'd say she's interesting looking. And in that sense, interest is a dangerous conceit — if that's the right word. How's that bump on her head?"

Rad scratched the pump head and checked the mirrors.

"It reminds me of a poem I did once," Moe continued, with what appeared to be a total lack of concern for the reflected images that surrounded him. "It reminds me of all the diagnostics that lead up to the poem's creation."

"You wrote a poem, Moe? When?"

"When has nothin' to do with it, Rad. It's a creation — eternal to me. A poem, okay?"

"Is it Miltonic?" Rad queried with what may have been perceived as unrestrained enthusiasm.

"Beats me. I'd say it's naturally aspirated though ... based on empirical ..." Moe shot an inquisitive look at Rad.

"That's a good word, Moe"

"... empirical research and observation."

"Go, Moe, go!" Rad said, feigning a hypothetical beat spirit of encouragement.

Moe inhaled deeply and changed gears to something less frantic. The engine settled down to 3 on the big dial.

Moe inhaled again, and commenced to recite:

"Sometimes it's the words,
or is it ?
Sometimes it's what you mean,
or is it ?
Sometimes it's just the scene,
... I mean.
Or is it ?
But always:
I am
that is the man
who can fix it.

But when it comes to love,
what is it ?"

The two high-velocity poets were silent for a few minutes, content with car noises and wind whistles as the big dial started to climb to 5 or 6.

"It's missing something, isn't it?" Moe tried eventually.

More wind whistles.

"Just the bongo drum, Moe."

CHAPTER 10

It was neon glowing.
Again, and again:
like reciprocal dancing
on a polished wrist pin.
So in the old days
when the angels dug in:
Were all those words there,
on the head of a pin?
Why, nothing for nothing
whatever they'd been.

several weeks later

Six aliens, illegal and fractionally foreign-planet types with motor-infested haircuts and outdated neckties, were commanding a corner at Larry's Limited Slip Café (it's differential!). Like a lot of people from tough planets, the aliens were fast drinkers and chain-linked smokers.

There sure seemed to be plenty of action in the alien corner. But Larry looked tired, confusing the Pump Boy: What did it feel like to be tired? A dreamy, disconnected state with reduced personal space and a shrunken physical being, a ... perhaps, almost total lack of intellectual momentum.

Rad had to ask twice for his beverage of choice.

Just as the specified beverage arrived, there was a noise outside that sounded like someone trying to park a giant vacuum cleaner powered by a super-charged outboard motor. There were snorts of aggressive power and chirping burps from the tyres.

It was Moe.

... and Moe's skateboard car: a combination of man and machine in a spectacle of unchangeable hubris ... or so it seemed.

A rectangle of white outdoor light appeared in the wall. Moe stepped through the light hole which disappeared behind him, and delicately, carom by carom, made his way to the Pump Boy.

"Rad, what it is?"

"What it is, Moe."

"Where ya at?"

Rad didn't answer. Sometimes Moe talked without really saying or meaning anything. Probably because he hadn't made his mind up yet. Rad was that way too — at least about making his bed. After all,

[19] TRPB 287.226.4512
A means of depicting three-dimensional designs on paper. European projection shows the views differently from the American drafting conventions.

[20] TRPB 985.332.1050
Not sure what Rad is thinking here, but the two-clutch system to which Moe is likely referring was indeed abandoned by Porsche racing.

[21] TRPB 825.285.1624
Actual parts in the transmissions of older Porsches. Rad appears to be captivated by the names, envisioning, as usual, something entirely different.

everything just got messed up later, didn't it?

The mechanic twisted past the Pump Boy and slipped into an empty chair at the alien table. Placemats were inverted and napkins came out. Moe and the motor-headed imports started to sketch technical details ... of what looked like [peering] ... some kind of mechanical doughnut. A torque converter? It seemed odd to Rad that the drawings were being done in European projection. [19] This was, after all ... where was he anyway?

Moe lit a cigar. It was the biggest, smokiest, and most intensely fragrant smoke at the table. The aliens quickly snuffed their Marlboros out of respect for the connoisseur.

How exactly were they writing anyway? Was it backwards ... or perhaps even inside out?

Hard to ascertain.

But so was the now forgotten sky: the cement pie.
The sad, cold cigarette butt dead ... shot in the head.

The Pump Boy caught himself, having almost drifted off and probably having missed some of Moe's power flow dialogue, and his clapping hands imitating the twin clutches again ... and all that, coming back into focus.

Larry was cleaning up the spill that had been induced by the near slumber: " 'Nother one, Rad?"

"Sure. Say, Larry, one of those hair people with Moe is eating his red napkin."

Larry peered across the Pump Boy's exaggeratedly padded shoulders and squinted towards the smoldering corner of the blue haze: "Nah ... No he isn't. It looks more like a placemat."

Larry was right. It was a placemat.

"Yeah, well, that's interesting. Larry, I think that Moe is wrong though ... about the two clutches. I think that the concept was abandoned." [20]

"Doesn't matter, Rad. Those guys are buyers: big time. They're not here for Moe's transmission stories. They're here for some big stuff, big. Some exotic export. I know the type"

"Moe's stories are rather interesting, Larry. Has he told you about the Synchromesh, about the spiders and the roller cage? [21] Neat, huh? About the finely machined Inner Race? No wonder the Aliens are interested."

A wet rag dropped onto the floor, just inches from Larry's pink sneakers: "You say what, Rad?"

"I ... ?" Pumped the kid, pointing to himself.

"Yeah ... You said somethin' about aliens?"

"Oh, well ... " Rad fumbled, not really interested in causing any undue apprehension, "It's ... uh ... just an expression."

Larry mumbled off into the mirror maze, his sneakers still squeaking.

22 TRPB 002.105.1010
This line, put in quotation marks by Campbell, is most certainly lifted from Rupert Brooke's 1914 poem, *The Dead*. Rad graffiti, in contrast to the main text, often takes a melancholy turn, balancing the childlike Rad world with something grave and hurtful. This selection in particular seems to mirror these two sides of life:

These hearts were woven of human joys and cares,
washed marvellously with sorrow, swift to mirth.
The years had given them kindness.
Dawn was theirs, and sunset,
and the colours of the Earth.
These had seen movement, and heard music;
known slumber and waking;
loved;
gone proudly friended;
felt the quick stir of wonder;
sat alone;
touched flowers and furs and cheeks.
All this is ended.

23 TRPB 405.776.0354
Psychological self-handicapping named after the French chess player who offered a pawn at the start of the game, thereby establishing a win-win situation for himself (if he lost, he had given the advantage).

24 TRPB 211.099.0065
The legal terms indicate that there might be some sort of battle over inheritance. Rad continues to confuse words that sound the same with evident disregard for what the true subject matter might be.

25 TRPB 540.098.0645
An estate in fee simple is not a place at all as imagined by Rad, of course, but an absolute inheritance, clear of any particular heirs. It would seem clear that Rad has some pretty significant inheritance, as an estate in fee simple is the highest estate known to law. "Shangri-la" of course is the mythical paradise of perpetual youth as described in the 1933 novel *Lost Horizons*.

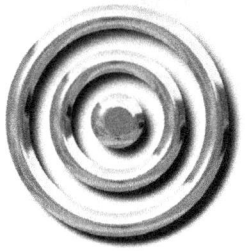

CHAPTER 11

"And sunset, and the colours of the Earth." [22]

A tear fell on the newspaper that he only imagined to be reading.

The Pump Boy shook his head.

Rad was playing back old newspaper headlines in his mind, most in condensed Gothic bold. It all started to add up. One day, at the supermarket he'd seen "ALIEN TRANSMISSIONS STARTED WWII!"

... an allegation that seemed to imply a lot more in the way of intergalactic automotive advances than those discussed in the very condensed article. The same was true of another headline that popped up several months later: "ALIEN SCIENCE ENDED WWII!"

The facts, Rad had often noticed, were always hard to distill ... no matter what the subject or what the source. I guess it could be called a sort of literary self-handicapping: "A Deschapelles coup for writers?" [23] pondered The Pump Boy.

Secretly, he thought that back in the days when books were copied by hand, there had probably been a greater control over a unified intellectual perspective, which of course, could have been what the aliens intended in the first place.

Some people never thought about books or aliens ... maybe antiquarians.

And most people never wanted to talk about aliens, so you had to be careful.

Hammering Jim, for example, didn't warm up to the subject at all. But Jim was usually off on some pretty weird subjects himself. Jim, it seemed, was incomprehensibly paranoid, always explaining in great mysterious detail how it was that everyone was out to get you. Get you from what?

Not that some of Jim's stories were not rather engaging, such as his version of the tortious and the heirs. [24] Or the various ramblings about negotiable instruments, which Rad presumed must look like trombones. Then there was Jim's explanation to Rad about Rad's estate in Fee Simple: Jim seemed to think it was very good indeed, and it sounded like a neat place to hang out. *Maybe like Shangri-La.* [25]

[26] TRPB 002.105.1010
Martin Heidegger, German
phenomenologist who studied
the problem of being, which
western culture had abandoned.
The graffito indicates that the
common notion of time is false:
that it is not a line, but spherical.
Breaking away from the
subject-object dichotomy.

[27] TRPB 002.105.1010
A musical direction used
primarily at the end of a
movement. It indicates a
gradual diminishing and
means "losing strength."

CHAPTER 12

Wired for sound that was wound around a transcendental line of time snipped into little pieces. Time was quiet, perhaps. Passing barely noticed, but certainly spherical. And so surgical, we thought, where is Heidegger now?[26]

burning, burning

At first there was nothing. No smell of smoke, no ring of translucent haze. No noise.

It was often like this: staring at the unfamiliar window skeleton without even a small piece of recognition. Then gradually The Pump Boy would remember that everything had an orientation, and, if looked at carefully enough, could be placed carefully into the puzzle. Things had to be remembered all over again ... in a matter of seconds.

It was often like this. But how often?

Rad had a headache. All he could think about was the window at first, and all he could remember was ... something very distant about aliens and flaming hairspray cans. Were they using the hairspray cans for blowtorches and burning each other up into sparkles of bright colours? Where did they get the illegal hairspray?

Larry had kicked everybody out. Unusual for him — out of character, you might say. But out of the bar for sure. There was something about KillFlash, too: Did he really pull a weapon on the chain-smoking aliens and ruin their party? What did KillFlash know about

aliens anyway? Was that what started the hairspray fight?

Rad made a mental note to learn some bad language someday, for times like this. If Moe had been there, he would have said a bad word.

Rad put his necktie on with extreme care ... or was it blithe disregard? Adjectives were such funny things, weren't they?

"Everyday starts the same," noted The Pump Boy, talking to the Alien spy in the mirror and wondering whether the Alien day was just ending. They both shrugged, "Perdendo le forze !" [27]

There was little use in polishing the Rambler's windscreen: The haze would last until noon, or thereabouts. Besides, the drive to the shop wound through the processing sector. The sector was always misty and filmy, the sky always dripped, potholes filled with silver pieces of sky tossed their coruscating contents back and forth, and all in all, whatever that means, it wasn't a good place to have a clean piece of glass anyway.

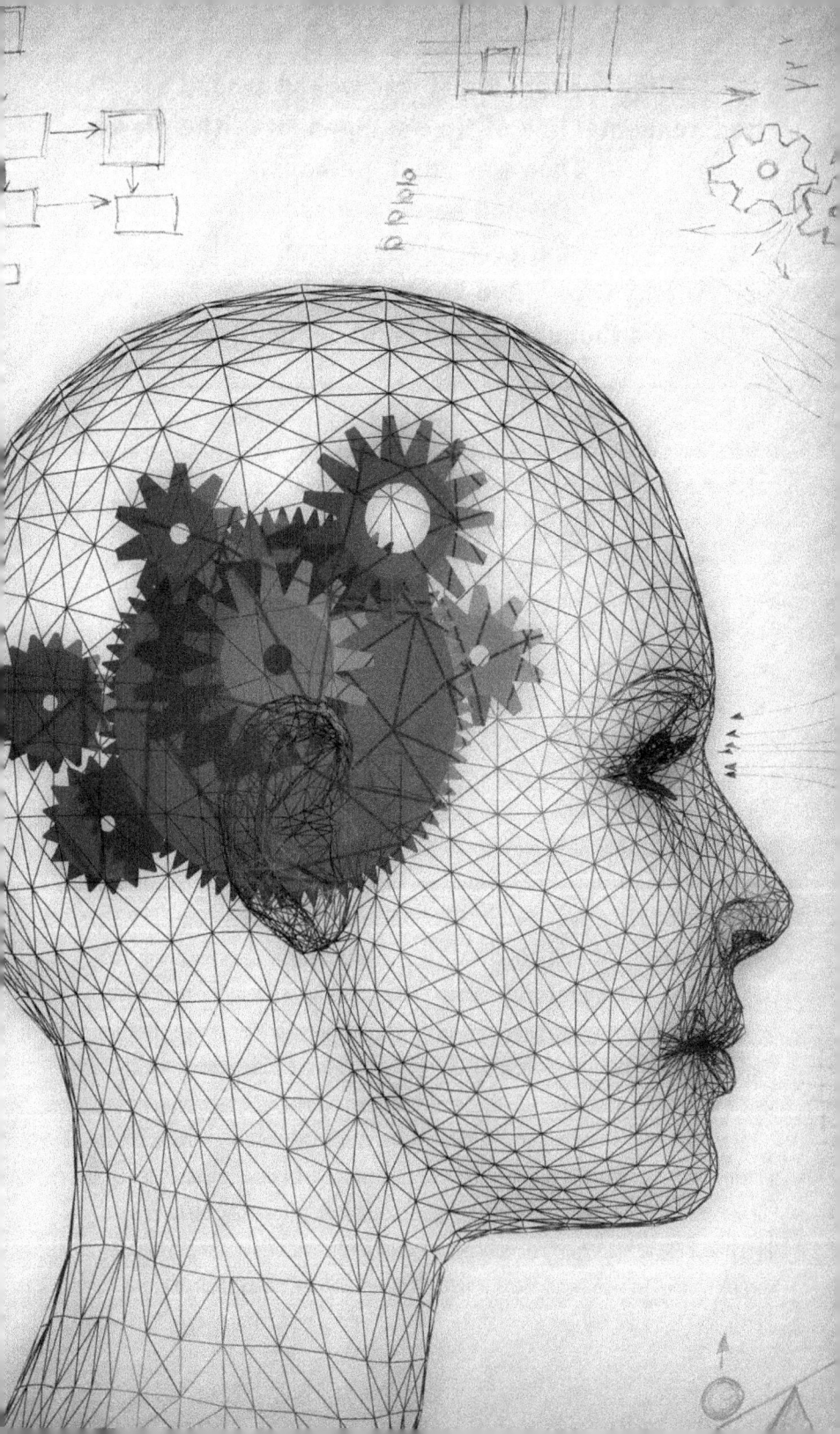

**windows rolled up tight.
Tough knuckle to bite.
Try as you might,
ya gotta fight.**

To get to the shop, you had to park on the sidewalk and descend a cast iron stairway to a basement door. Rad appreciated what had been called the exaggerated gothic atmosphere of the entrance, or, well, the whole block, for that matter. Wealthy people had once lived here, and it had been their practice, allegedly, to build reproductions of buildings that were built by people who had been even wealthier in the days of greater individual wealth ... or something like that. It never really made a great deal of sense, even if you thought about it. But there was plenty of stone and a lot of pretty good carving, cast iron, leaded windows — no doubt leftover doodles produced by artistic immigrants.

Rad was glad to have such neat-looking buildings around.

He was glad too, to see the neat-looking car that Largo Lips drove sleeping on the curb outside the shop. The car looked something like Moe's skateboard car but much bigger, blacker, and more like a spaceship, or more like something designed to look like a spaceship. Definitely not from this planet. Anybody could see that. Like Moe's car, it had sleepy eyes and no hood ornament, no radiator grill, and a very smooth line from front to back. The rear tyres were barely visible. Each eye had two lenses in it, one of which was looking around the corner because the front wheels were turned that way ... a pretty neat

51

[28] TRPB 108.224.0001
The famous French Citroën is (very accurately) described here — either a DS or SM. The height of the car was adjusted through the use of a hydro-pneumatic suspension; typically, older cars would "leak down" when parked, lowering themselves to within inches of the ground. And yes, the headlights did turn with the steering wheel.

[29] TRPB 132.532.9835
Undeniably a reference to the hypnotic scene from Jean Cocteau's 1949 film *Orpheus*, in which Orpheus, wearing special gloves, passes through into the underworld by walking through a mirror. The scene was made possible by using a large vat of mercury. This is a continuation of the mirror theme into deep esoterica.

[30] TRPB 196.961.5209
Another film from the '60s, (1966) *Blow-Up* is about a photographer who thinks he sees an image of a murder taking place in a photograph that he has taken (as he blows it up). Interesting exploration of what is real, what is unreal.

[31] TRPB 362.465.9785
"We're expecting company."

feature. And the car would go to sleep when parked, slowly sinking lower and lower to the ground as it relaxed. [28]

The basement itself was a maze of steaming, oozing pipes and humming power conduits. There were unidentifiable pools of liquid dotted about the floor — some of the liquid radiated an opalescent glow. Some of it looked like pools of mercury mirrors waiting to be entered with rubber gloves [29] — as if to grasp another world — the underworld. Or was this the underworld? Two wide, parallel yellow stripes on the floor flanked the angular pathway that led to the repair shop, a subterranean glass store front, behind which a lady with very brown hair and very brown eyes was polishing a gleaming piece of brass. It looked like gold. But it was brass.

Her hair was cut in a manner of a sophisticated 1960s look ... very difficult to get just right. It was damp, too, as usual. There was nothing fuzzy or big about her hair, and she had her own fingernails: two-toned pink translucence. She reminded Rad of Vanessa Redgrave in the movie *Blow-Up*.[30] There was a minor employment problem rooted in the fact that the lady spoke no English ... or even American.

Rad smiled at her and looked at the musical instrument parts lined up artistically on the counters:

"These are lovely. What a nice job. Thank you."

"Nous attendons du monde," [31] she said, glancing up at the ceiling.

Rad looked up too, but he didn't see anything. He did hear the bell on the front door and wondered whether it might be a customer

Hammering Jim slid through the door and scowled. He was wearing a tan trench coat (Rad's was black).

"I've got to get this inventory thing cleared up, Rad. Even though the bank guys wouldn't know a trumpet from a strumpet, I happen to know trash from cash. So I wanna see the active inventory at least. Where is this stuff?"

Rad looked searchingly at Jim, wondering what exactly either Jim or the bankers knew about music. Or maybe he was really concluding rather than thinking. But ... what was the difference? And ... what was a strumpet?

"They're all back here, Jim. The good stuff. It's the real thing."

³² TRPB 645.902.9531
The names on the crates correspond to the
names of the stops (those long pipes that
rise up behind a full-size pipe organ) A universal
air chest is a system for supplying a full and
steady flow of pressurized air to the organ
stops; it is superior to the concussion bellows
and was introduced in the 1890s.

³³ TRPB 503.665.1069
Legal terms that Rad must be confusing with a
more exotic subject, tales of adventure perhaps.
One term refers to the withdrawal of goods shipped
to an insolvent vendee; the *Ultra Vires* is an act
beyond a corporation's defined powers.
Both could apply here.

The crates

The crates were tremendous, oaken boxes, each clearly stenciled with mysterious manifestos of their contents.

Some crates were short and square, while others were elongated, such as the one marked *Fagotto*, which appeared to contain torpedoes. There was one as long as two automobiles, a huge crate, marked *Open and Stopped Diapason*. and another, just as long, labeled *Sub Bourdon*, on top of which was a crate about eight feet long, interestingly stenciled, *Voix Celeste. Vox Humana. Cor-de-Nuit.* [32]

These were no ordinary shipping crates. They were outfitted with brass hardware and lacquered oak timber. They were heavy; they were old. They were locked, and they went on and on, forming the walls of a maze the size of a small house.

Jim was apprehensive, "Look at this crap. It must be a million years old. The auditors won't buy this again, Rad. You gotta move this dead inventory out of here. It's as active as a mummy in a sealed tomb." Jim looked around, wrinkling his brow and pursing his lips. "This place gives me the creeps, Rad. Even if it had active inventory, it would still give me the creeps."

"Jim, there's a big difference between a concussion bellows system and a universal air chest. The air chest is what attracted me to this opportunity in the first place."

"The line of credit doesn't recognize the difference, Rad. You're so far into the bank with this stuff that you're going to move something one way or another. What am I supposed to tell them? That you got a great deal on a 16th-century pipe organ?"

"It was a good deal, but it's not really that old. Not even half that old."

"It doesn't matter. What matters is whether you can sell it for more than you paid for it. Or just sell it at all. Hell, I don't care."

"It's not for sale, Jim. You know that. I think that the creeps must be bad for you. Why don't we talk about *Stoppage in Transito* or that *Ultra Vires act*?" [33]

"That might not be a bad idea. But every time I refresh your memory, you rearrange it again."

"I used to do that a lot when I was a kid: I'd move, say, the desk over to the window, maybe change the direction of the bed and hang pictures in different ways. Always the same stuff: but in new places, in new ways.

34 TRPB 115.787.6598
French phenomenologist who wrote
La poétique de l'space in the '50s.
It's about the reality of the space, such
as drawers, cabinets, rooms, that we
create. It would seem that The Pump
Boy has read the book. Phenomenological themes are employed extensively
by Campbell (see Bachelard's
introduction).

35 TRPB 005.892.1068
"One of these days."

36 TRPB 315.192.9988
This seems to be a combination
of advice from both painters. Van Gogh
did write to his brother, Theo, about
painting the essential.

I'd clean up a little too. It was sort of like creating a new existence, phenomenologically speaking, of course. But it wouldn't be the same if you thought about it that way. Have you ever read Gaston Bachelard's *Poetics of Space*?" [34]

Jim stared at Rad, at Rad's necktie, specifically, which appeared to have been crudely shortened to sternum length. Rad was looking around the shop, smiling quietly while visualizing a new arrangement for the crates.

"Are you listening to me, Rad?"

"Absolutely, Jim."

"Let's get outta here. My car's getting coated with goop."

They passed through the front of the shop, dodging instruments that were hanging from an invisible, flat black ceiling.

Rad smiled at Largo Lips.

"... *un de ces jours, Radis,*" she said. [35]

Jim pulled The Pump Boy through the door. "She just called you a radish."

"So what do you expect, Jim? She doesn't speak English."

* * *

Jim's glop-covered car splashed down off the sidewalk and shrank away through the architectural tunnel of crumbling stone. The earthbound spots of cement sky rippled in his wake. The car disappeared quietly: it was always quiet everywhere now.

Rad walked toward the trunk of the Rambler and looked at the bulky assortment of papers that Jim had given to him. All the printing was on one side. Great: plenty of drawing room.

"I'll call this one A Crystal Window's View of the Street."

Rad flipped the paper stack over and placed it on the Rambler's trunk. A crayon skidded back and forth, waxing an ever-tangling network of bold lines and seemingly suggestive line quality.

He paused, changed crayon colours, and made a terminal squiggle ... completing the activity with an artist's final flourish of resolve.

It was a neat drawing. But upon looking up, Rad noted that the masterpiece didn't accurately sum up the landscape — no, not at all, in fact. But isn't that what Van Gogh said: Don't paint what you can see, paint the essential ... or something like that ... or was that Pissarro? [36]

"Oh well," he said, opening the trunk and tossing the papers inside to join dozens of others, "Maybe I'll call it something else. There's always another name for something."

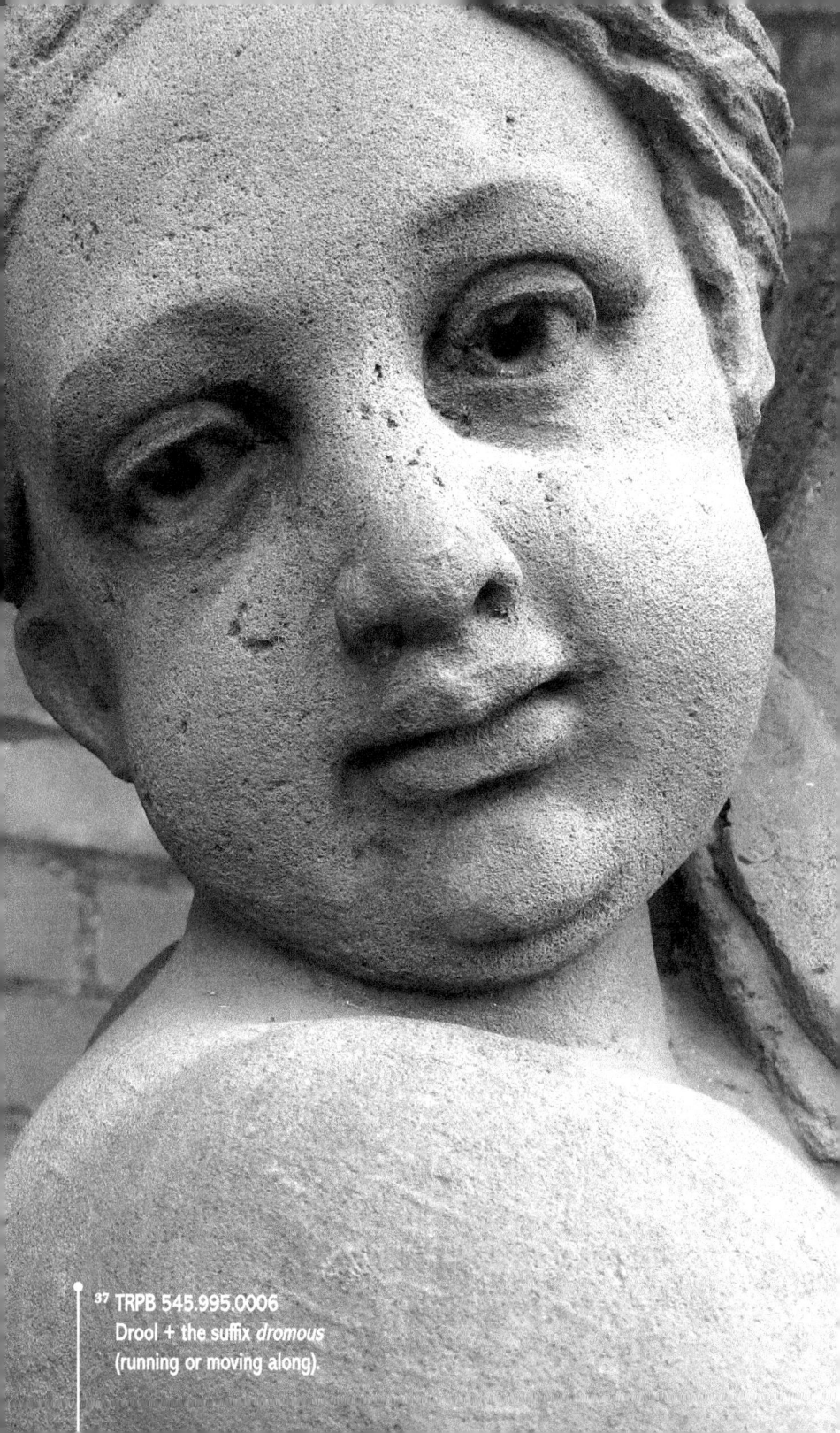

[37] TRPB 545.995.0006
Drool + the suffix *dromous*
(running or moving along).

statues stare
forever
drooldromous[37] sky ... why ?

Slithering debris coated the road: nomadic hordes of paper, plastic, and metallic rabble washed back and forth in hurried waves. The wash made the road surface slippery, though, and presented a minor road hazard.

Billboard faces watched the lone Rambler, which was still green, and now, covered with a morning drool of goop.

Visibility was poor.

The mirrors were covered too, effectively blocking alien transmissions. Thus the intergalactic communication channels were foiled, and the exact whereabouts of nourishing paper products, cardboard, and red fruit, inadvertently sheltered from probing alien inquiries.

That was at least one possibility.

Rad was thinking about the number of possibilities that could exist, if one were to entertain the proposition of a universal eternity ... or was it eternal universe ... or infinity? Yes, that was it: an infinite universe in space and time. It seemed to make sense that a universe without an end would contain every possible imaginable situation. Which would lead to every possible imaginable outcome ... and probably a whole lot more. Of course, with half of the street signs missing, and the roads a little confusing and unfamiliar, it seemed a better idea to convert the mind back to functioning as the Rambler's brain.

It was no bother, really:
Rad didn't mind sharing.

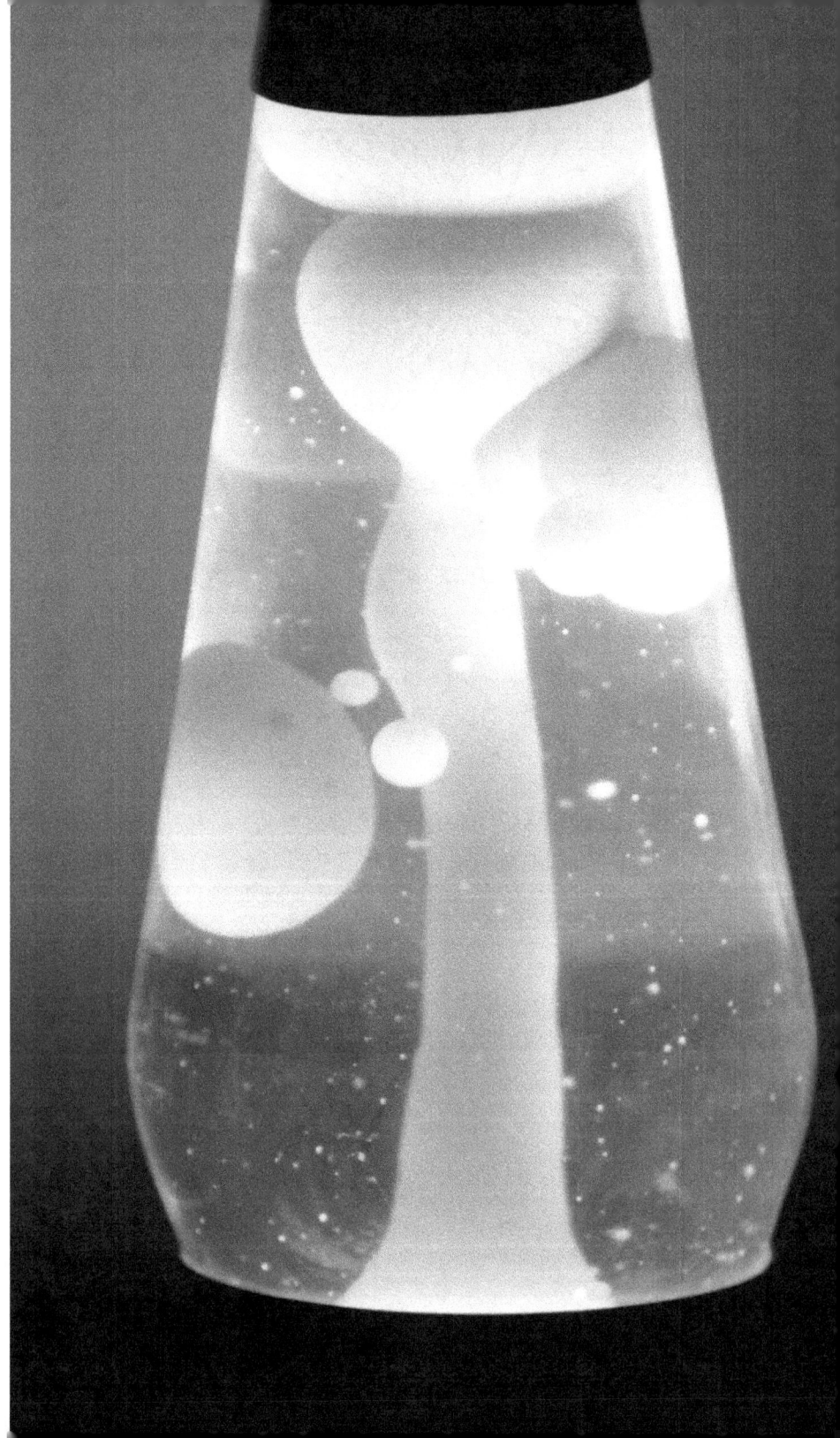

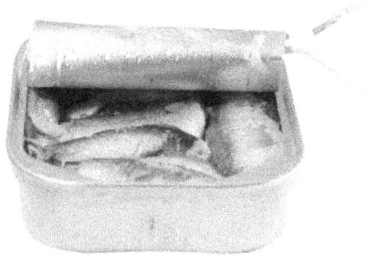

CHAPTER 16

In with the bright lights.
Out with the smoke.
They say:
that's all he wrote

With only a few small but interesting delays, The Pump Boy found his way to the garage, which seemed to radiate a particularly intense resplendence.

Moe had been decorating again. Somehow the concrete island on which the gas pumps hung out appeared to float a few inches off the ground, suspended by an intense pink glow. In a way, it looked sort of eerie, but then again, it also looked normal. Maybe Moe had hot-wired them as well.

"Morning, Rad," Moe said, interrupting the concentrated awe. "Neat, huh ? You gotta see it at night: Looks great. I did it with neon tubing under the apron, see ..."

Moe kicked at the glow with his boot. The glow made a metallic clunking sound, which didn't seem glow-like, though just what kind of sounds photons were supposed to make had always been a mystery to The Pump Boy.

"It's sort of a new look ... for a new era," Moe said, staring along with Rad.

"Moe, I've seen cars driving around with this kind of glow. Isn't it kind of an old thing? Or maybe what I'm thinking is ... (longish pause). What new era, Moe? Have I missed something?"

"I think so, Rad. You know, your girlfriend came by and dropped off your lava lamp ... she said you dumped her. You had a fight about music? How does that happen?

"So I sorta figured you were clued into the situation."

"Oh," Rad said, "I was thinking more about the new era, Moe, and missing that."

"Isn't this your lamp, Rad?" Moe held out a plastic cylinder full of multi-coloured oil for Rad's inspection. The electrical cord was plugged into Moe's belt for, well ... whatever

reason: but either way, the light didn't seem to be functioning properly.

"Well ... I, uh ... That's a cool lamp, Moe. But I don't think it's mine. And I don't understand the dumping thing ..."

"I know, Rad: You just forgot. If I were you, I'd take the lamp and keep forgetting the whole thing. If you didn't think that you were supposed to have a girlfriend, you wouldn't have one anyway. Young men don't have clear wants. Guys like me ... " (there was a self-acknowledging and, it seemed, introspective shrug), "We have clear wants."

Rad began to wonder what it was that Moe was talking about. He didn't seem to be himself ... talking about clarity as if it could be anything other than some kind of vague vision or concoction found in a self-help book. Moe just didn't seem right. Well, except for the neon trick. But the girl talk — if you could call it that — was not a normal part of the Moe repertoire.

The Pump Boy inspected the master mechanic: He looked normal, he smelled the same, his cigar was of the normal variety, and he was shifting his weight back and forth ever so slightly from one leg to the other ... which ... was ... also normal.

"Moe, I already have a lamp just like this."

Moe's face was glowing in slow, cigar-illuminated pulsations: light on, then smoke out; light on, then smoke out — sort of an in with the bright lights, out with the smoke.

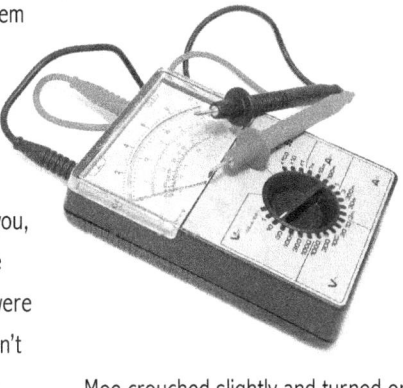

Moe crouched slightly and turned on his heel, very much creating the appearance of being on a skateboard. He zoomed off in the direction of the open garage bay with uncharacteristic speed. The trail of cigar smoke, viewed under such circumstances, reminded the Pump Boy of the vapour trail behind a jet, even though it was really following a Hawaiian shirt.

Rad thumped the glowing neon apron with his sneaker and produced a satisfying and melodious tone that was suitably glow-like.

There was no response from the photons, which was to be expected. But this led to a brief contemplation of the age-old question: how could something with no mass possess momentum?

Maybe they're just carriers?

Rad followed the jet stream into the garage, where Moe was standing underneath a brown car.

"Say, Moe. What do you know about photons?"

"Huh? ... Well, the usual, just like everybody else."

"Couldn't you say that photons are actually carriers of energy rather than the energy itself?"

"I think you're talking about pheromones, Rad. Pheromones are kinda like nitrous oxide."

Rad shrugged.

The science was obviously arcane, and Moe was busy, staring in that slightly puzzled, slightly all-knowing way of his at some part that had a lot of tubes coming out of it. The tubes went to different locations within the car, and the whole scene was in black-and-white ... well, except for Moe's face, which was changing colours, and, in a way, dimensions, sometimes looking like Moe, sometimes looking like something that the Rad had never seen before.

"When you look at something for more than a few seconds, Moe, ever notice how it how it keeps changing and sort of visually breathing. . .breathing in and out of reality, how it just doesn't look real anymore? Well, it looks real enough: it's just that the image is

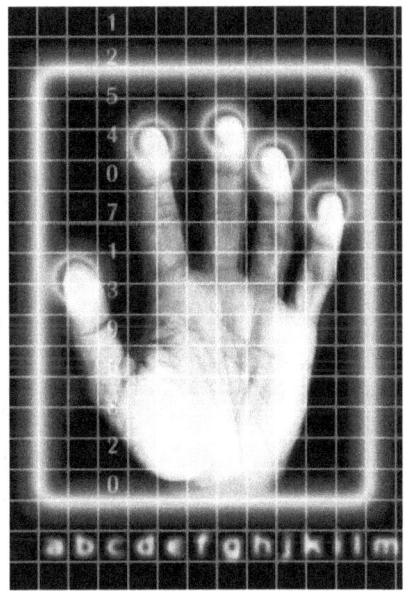

constantly squirming around in your mind ... sort of a tossing and turning of puzzling images ... trying to find a safe, recognizable pattern to talk to, to link with ... but somehow it never does? "

Moe turned to The Pump Boy, and starting at floor level, made a complete visual inspection of the kid right on up to the hair tips, which were fully extended vertically, almost electrically, out of the Rad head. Moe knitted his brow ever so slightly and took in a puff of bright lights. He seemed to be focused on the tips of Rad's quill-like hair .

"Yeah," Moe said, "... I've noticed that."

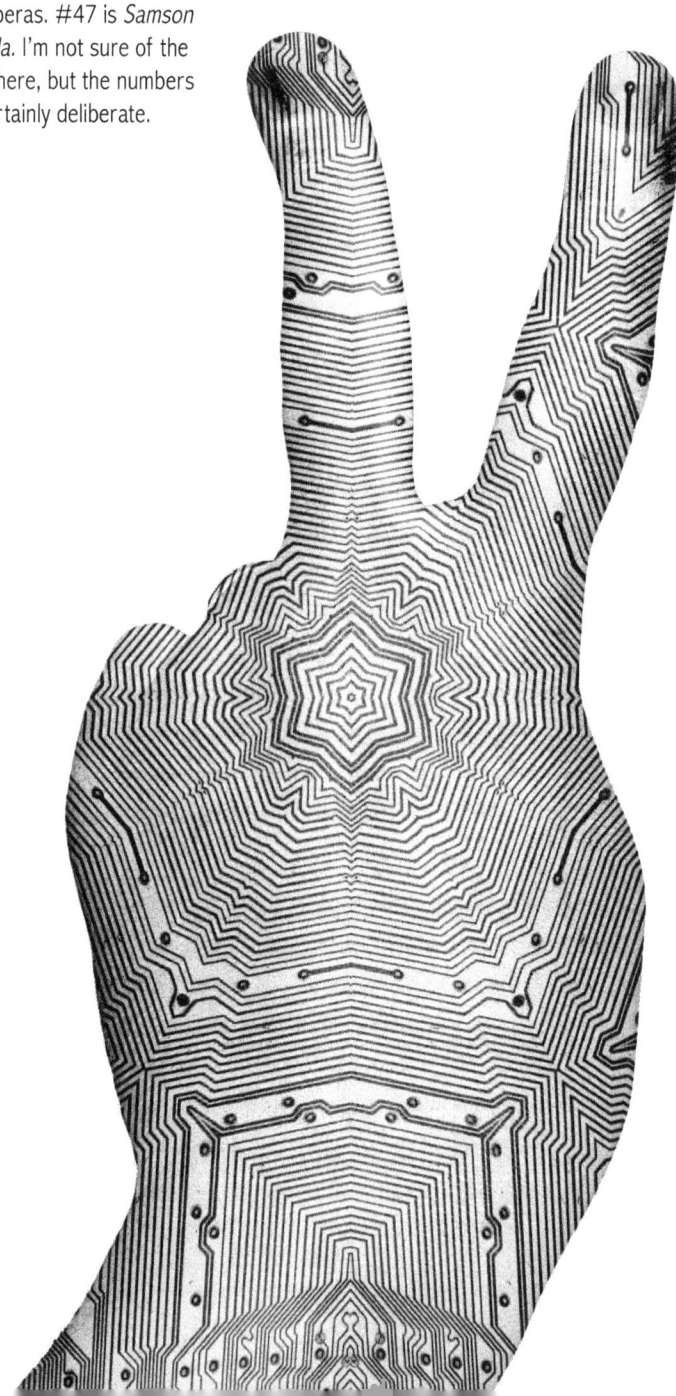

38 TRPB 002.105.1010
Opus number 30 of *Saint-Saëns*,
an opera. Interestingly, the other
numbers mentioned relate to
opus #45 and 47, which are
also operas. #47 is *Samson
et Dalila*. I'm not sure of the
intent here, but the numbers
are certainly deliberate.

Chapter 17

Bad canned heat of the day
trickled so did it like a little Bo Peep:
Her red-hot waves come closing range
and ray gun magnums for Champagne stains.

Listen up!
Our attention is sinking.
It's a whirlpool of sand.
Spilling from your hand.

Rad graffito

Rad was thinking about a toy airplane that he once had as a kid.

It was just a stick of balsa wood with a red plastic propeller on one end and a rubber band in the middle. The band ran lengthwise below the stick to a spot just in front of the tail fins. There was also a plastic clip that held the wings in place on the stick ... or fuselage, as pilots call it. There were some neat graphics on the wings that were supposed to intimate the appearance of a jet; and even though they weren't very convincing, they still looked cool. Elaborate assembly and operation instructions were written on the package. The instructions explained that the young Rad was to carefully count 30 turns of the propeller while winding it in preparation for flight.

Rad had counted the 30 turns. But he felt the increasing resistance of the rubber band and kept going, wanting to store even more energy for the maiden flight. "La Princesse Jaune" [38] was playing in his head as a musical score for the monumental event. He continued counting, and pressing onward, pacing himself with the music and passing 45 revolutions easily, and then at 47 ... as the hand moved ... the music changed.

That's when it happened.
That's when the balsa fuselage snapped.
There was just a handful of splinters and a big knot of writhing rubber band.

And that was it.

In retrospect, it could have happened to anyone. But then again, it hadn't happened to anyone. It had happened to Rad.

And that was that.

This, concluded The Pump Boy at a very early age, was pretty much how things work, maybe all things, maybe all philosophies. Yes, Rad was thinking, sometimes life is just a broken toy airplane that never flew. What came before, what came after ... it was all the same experience over and over again. Like listening to Chopin.

An overhead shriek interrupted the somber contemplation of things past and things permanent. Rad glanced up and caught a glimpse of a sharpened shimmer of high-speed flash across the leaky yellow sky. Or, he thought, growing optimistic perhaps, sometimes life is an alien spacecraft that nobody else sees.

The Pump Boy shrugged and lurched awkwardly in the direction of the goo-coated Rambler. Cars were coming in to drink gas, and the station was beginning to look busy. Moe had to break his concentration on the tubing thing and serve the cars. Moe always had an interesting crowd, and served a wide variety of car beverages: some cars — well, the people inside actually — asked for both gas and nitrous oxide. Some mixed various amounts of the different fuels. All of the cars made lots of noise, which was unusual for cars in general, but seemed to be almost the standard for Moe's car friends. Most of them made a raspy whirring noise ... somewhat related perhaps to the sound of an air-powered dental drill, but not as constant. There was always an up-and-down, nervous staccato rhythm. Sort of like two tomcats having a territorial dispute and using dental drills for voices. Well, only in this case, there were a whole bunch of tomcat cars, all pawing readily at the blacktop, squirming from spot to spot, warming up perhaps for an impressive exit, one that was always conducted in a grand wail of fortissimo and high spirits.

The scene, though full of colour and action, created a strange feeling in the Radical stomach ... or at least, in that part of the body where Rad presumed that the stomach was located. It was a slightly uneasy feeling: like something was missing.

Rad looked down, noting that nothing appeared to be missing and that everything seemed to be in order. Except for the shoe combination, which in addition to being what could be called a mismatch, was also illegal. The left shoe — or was it the right? — was part of the Known Water Authority uniform, and, as such, was not permissible as off-duty wear.

But the shoe thing couldn't be related to the missing thing.

Whatever was missing wasn't anything like a shoe.

Rad continued to drift until he bumped into the Rambler, mildly startled.

Maybe what was missing was some form of fuel? Rad looked back at the bright colours and elaborate staging of the hungry skateboard cars. This was their world, and Rad knew that he couldn't have a drink with them, just like he couldn't talk to aliens ... or even talk to Largo Lips, for that matter.

The missing-part feeling began to expand. Rad ignited the trusty Rambler and slid away from the lot, in the quiet gliding rumble of the old car world.

The world outside looked the same again, as usual. A bit of a disappointment, perhaps. After all, when one is experiencing a different sort of feeling, it's unnerving to be in a typical situation, on a typical street, under a typical sky, on a typical day ... or even to recognize these things as such. But then, there was never very far to go or much to do that didn't start looking unfamiliar: like déja vu that you had forgotten about, scattered about your life, piecing and bonding two realities together like cosmic stitching, or sometimes like an occasional phenomenological adhesive.

The Pump Boy spotted a street that he had never been on before and entered it after having waved the appropriate hand signal. The world around him slowly lost its colour and became monochromatic dinge.

"It's a black and white movie out there," observed The Pump Boy, noting that only he and his car had been filmed in colour. Chromatically speaking, it was a scene of parallel universes passing each other, or, at least, that was one way it could be viewed, but without the aforementioned stitching or glue.

In the distance, he could see what appeared to be a large ornamental fountain: it was several blocks away, perhaps. It stood in a mirage of colour, the water spray evidently rinsing the black and white from everything within its range. There were very few fountains anywhere these days, so it seemed odd.

The fountain itself even seemed odd, which was now an appropriate feeling. And the water pressure was unusual. Rad had some knowledge of water and The Water Authority — well, more precisely, he knew what valves to turn at what times and how to disconnect the phone — so it seemed like a good idea to investigate the fountain

[39] TRPB 267.445.9259
A play on Romance languages, esp. French. The meaning is clear (French explorers either colonised outer space or they were colonising the Earth). There is a play on the difference in French between "inter" and "entre." A general translation: *Intergalactic automobile, no passing.*

phenomenon. Plus, it seemed like a good idea for the two scenes filmed in colour to merge within the black and white universe ... or something like that.

Rad downshifted to slow his approach. Quiet spray began to accumulate on the front window of the Rambler. Some of the remaining goo began to change colour in litmus hues of pink and blue. Rad switched on the windshield wipers, only to produce a relatively uniform smear of translucent pale violet.

"Cool!," said The Pump Boy, "Well ... kind of," just after bumping into something that brought the Rambler to a relaxed halt.

The spray was now surprisingly intense, and a continued application of the wiper mechanism was slowly removing the violet translucence and producing a clear view of the circumstances.

The circumstances were, of course, unusual. At least for Rad. But the story that they told was clear.

The fountain was nothing more than a trite image of urban decay and neglect: a fire hydrant that had been sheared off at street level. Nothing unusual there, except — well, as a professional observation — the unusually high and consistent water pressure. But sitting just beyond the hydrant was the obviously culpable device: a large, heavy-looking machine with the appearance of an overgrown crêpe pan. It was about the size of three or four automobiles, and it didn't have wheels. There were small portholes along what appeared to be the top and some decorative symbols painted on the partly scorched bright silver sides.

Spacecraft, all right. Probably made of titanium and hafnium ... or maybe of something that hadn't been invented yet.

Stenciled on the rear were the letters VOITURE ENTRE-GALLACTIQUÉ, and in smaller letters, INTERDIT De DOUBLÉ ... an interesting bit of intergalactic argot that had evolved in the sphere of space and time. [39]

Rad thought about getting out of the car so that he could examine the giant crashed crêpe pan, perhaps peer into the portholes and check out the control panel. He wondered whether it was an automatic or stick shift. But unfortunately, The Pump Boy couldn't forget the frightening scene from the movie *The Man From Planet X*, in which an inquisitive and intrepid onlooker peered into a similar porthole only to be confronted with the bizarre face of the man from Planet X, sweating profusely and wearing what appeared to be a diver's

[40] TRPB 122.009.7536
There really is such a, '50s sci-fi movie (1951), and it is unusually atmospheric, taking place on a misty Scottish island. The interesting parallel here is that the scientist in the movie cannot figure out whether the alien is a friend or foe (since they can't communicate). Worth a watch.

[41] TRPB 016.994.1255
The father of electronic music. *Drone*, recorded in the '50s is an impressive, imaginative, and intensely brave composition: not for the faint-hearted. Bizarre. A trail blazer.

mask. Well, actually, the problem was that Rad couldn't quite remember exactly what happened in the movie,[40] and since this was the only scene from the movie that he could even vaguely remember, he felt somewhat apprehensive about exploring the blank screenplay. Anything could happen, and his experiences had led him to conclude that it usually did.

Or would someday.

He could always come back at another time ... maybe when it wasn't raining. Of course it wasn't raining everywhere. Behind him, for example, sitting on a parklike bench in the rearview mirror was a hurdy-gurdy man. He was merely sitting in a bordering mist. It was rather odd, Rad thought: a hurdy-gurdy man sitting in such a lonely spot, not even playing his instrument, which was really a barrel organ ... even though everyone called them hurdy-gurdies. He wondered what ever happened to the monkey. Maybe that was what had gone wrong. People said that the hurdy-gurdy man would talk to his monkey when he played the barrel organ. Even though there wasn't a monkey. But what do people really know about a monkey that they can't even see?

The Pump Boy sat quietly in the Rambler. Over the light patter of water droplets and drifting spray, there was an ever-so-faint metallic ticking sound that could barely be heard over the hissing drone of the Rambler's V-belts. Rad actually recognized and labeled the sounds: Hissing drone and Metallic ticking, noting that they worked in a kind of admirable symphonic simplicity seldom found outside of the works of Dockstator,[41] whose most spellbinding work was coincidentally christened *Drone*.

Rad shifted the Rambler into reverse and backed away from the wreckage, marveling at life's little coincidences ... whatever they were.

Upon arriving home, The Pump Boy was greeted by Fuzzy, a girlfriend from what seemed like ... an awfully long time ago.

Ribbons of blue smoke rose from the gaps between her skin and clothing, mostly around the neck, the ribbons rising up like charmed snakes, slowly soaring a foot or two and disintegrating into a ceiling-hugging cloud.

She looked like confusion bottled under pressure.

Rad sat down. He could still hear the

metallic ticking, which, well, as was pretty obvious, was coming from the old wrist-watch he often wore. It didn't sound the same without the Rambler's belt hiss. "So aren't you going to ask about how I've been? Or are you gonna start with C-flat again?" — queried the smoldering ex.

"I saw the strangest thing today ..." started The Pump Boy.

"I'm talking to you about my state of mind, here. But you're interested in talking about something strange you saw? Isn't that what you see every day? Do you see anything that isn't strange? You listen to whales talk to each other. Or to music that has to be flat or minor, or whatever that stuff is. You don't even know what planet you're on!" Good point, Rad thought.

The Fuzzy-headed girl was up now and moving toward the door, "You're hope-less. And how can you live in a place with no door lock? Anybody could walk in here anytime and steal everything you own." She passed through the door, trailing, "From the looks of it, somebody already did."

Rad was still thinking about planets. They had relationships, too.

Moe had once said that the horror of ending a relationship was the inverse of the fascination of starting one. And though that sounded mathematically inarguable and philosophically engaging, The Pump Boy could only think that all of his experiences seemed rather accidental and that it was decidedly difficult to ascertain what was the beginning and what was the end. To him, it seemed similar to the hurdy-gurdy man in the rearview mirror: What exactly is a hurdy-gurdy man when he is not playing his hurdy-gurdy? Is it about the monkey? Was he just in it for the monkey? Who was working for whom? Where had they all gone? The hurdy-gurdies, the icemen, pirates, and all the phone booths?

There was a demonstrational slam of the door a few floors below, at street level. Rad could hear the click-click-click of heels through the window. He liked that sound — coming or going. Could it be that some sounds are pheromonal?

The Pump Boy shrugged. What was wrong with whale songs anyway? And who really knew what planet he was on anyway? Hind-sight is twenty-twenty, right? Or was it? What difference did it make which way you looked since it is all the same? You think about the future, and you have no idea what is going to happen — you just think that you do. Then you reflect on the past, and, confound it, you have no idea what happened there either — you just think that you do.

Maybe it was a good time to walk down to Larry's for a beer.

[42] TRPB 302.195.4565
The "escapement" is the part
of a clock that makes the ticking
sound. Rubies are often used
on the pallet, which is the part
that shuttles back and forth
to make the ticking sound.

[43] TRPB 589.336.3562
This appears to be another
reference to Martin Heidegger's
work.

CHAPTER 18

Escapement Blues:
The thought was a tick, or was it a tock.
Or just a couple of rubies
who really want to rock...
the pallet of the clock. [42]

It seemed that a long time had passed since Rad had been to Larry's, maybe even a week. And Larry's was the kind of place that changed faces regularly, maybe every week.

Or maybe he just forgot.

Sure, there were the usual locals. But there was something oddly foreign about the crowd. It was hard to see back through the smoke, and even harder to hear any particular conversation, but it was pretty obvious that Officer KillFlash was having a heated discussion with a group of particularly odd-looking patrons. Rad shimmied over to the bar and asked Larry about the interrogation.

"Don't get started with anything, Rad. Whatever it is, it's none of our business. Don't you think I have enough trouble in here without you getting everybody worked up about those guys? They're just guys, Rad. They look funny and act weird, sure. But it's just a question of when, you know, for everybody in here. We all get weird sooner or later."

"We don't all look weird," Rad tried, attempting to call attention to the fact that these guys didn't just look weird. They looked, in fact, very damn weird — extremely weird, even to him.

"Sure we do." Larry said, placing an overflowing mug in front of The Pump Boy.

"You know," Larry said, "to the bar it's all just atmosphere, something that's always happening, and connected, but also something that we can't fully figure out ... in terms of relating to it."

Rad scratched at the quill-like hair.

Larry continued: "It's like a doorknob on a door."

Rad scratched again, this time a little more frantically, and once more Larry summed up his perspective:

"A philosopher once said that the doorknob knows the feel of many hands. You ever heard that?"

"Well, no," Rad said, pushing the now-empty mug back to Larry for refueling. "I like the sound of it, though. And the phenomenological aspects are entertaining."

"Entertaining? Those aspects cannot be questioned ... for certainly the doorknob knows the feel of many hands. And the many hands clutch ignorantly, but purposefully; unthinkingly, but accurately. They do it because they want something on the other side. It is done out of expectation." [43]

"Beer, please," reflected The Pump Boy, wondering about the other side.

CHAPTER 19

The rabid track
drainage ditch deep green
filled with an insane scene
all wait, listening
the creaking door
a very voice du jour
rust in pain
or more.

the rabid track:
click clack
click clack
all fear
that it's the same rap
rat-ta-tat-tat.
Thought it was a heart attack.

Rad awoke to imagined strains of a country and western ballad in G-major.

"The shoeshine agony boy was in a hurry,
but he was such a fittin' one to worry.
In a face full of ag-o-nize-ing polish ...
he's jus' a'waitin' 'round for what he knew."

That was too close to a nightmare. Maybe better than a sea chanty. The Radical mind contemplated while checking the nightstand for a glass of water that was free of matchbooks. The days were starting to look the same, feel the same, maybe even be the same.

The Pump Boy started to miss the frightening glow of dawn. But it would be there. What else could be there be?

Oh, well, I guess that it could be anything. Late at night, things take on an unreal flavour: everyone starts to look like, and act like, an alien. All spaces become unfamiliar late enough at night.

Nothing makes any sense. But ... what time was it anyway?

Was it even late at night?

Rad couldn't remember, and he had forgotten how to figure it out — the procedure.

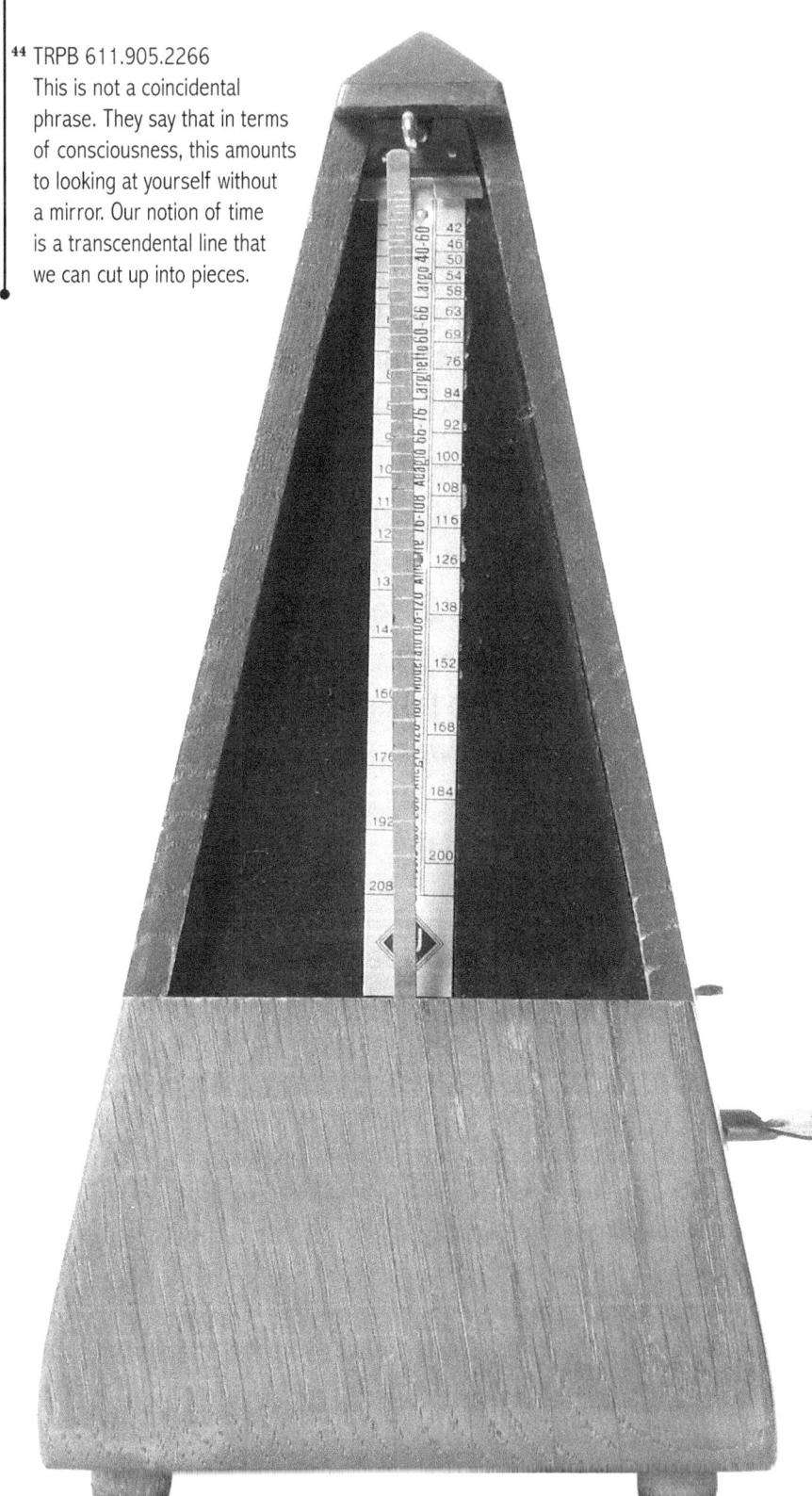

44 TRPB 611.905.2266
This is not a coincidental
phrase. They say that in terms
of consciousness, this amounts
to looking at yourself without
a mirror. Our notion of time
is a transcendental line that
we can cut up into pieces.

The darkness looked like an ornate tapestry with pointillistic accents, a kaleidoscopic pattern that filtered everything into an organic monster of vision that bore through all, twisting its frightening stained-glass colours into the very fabric of dreams that you were not even having — or were you?

Rad was still awakening and thinking, *"The shoeshine agony boy was in a hurry, but he was such a fittin' one to worry."*

This was no longer a dream. This was today. There was a lot to do, too — he was pretty sure about that. And, oh yeah, the phone booth on the corner: it wasn't there any more. Just gone. There were fewer and fewer phone booths around. So how was he supposed to call the shop?

Well, I guess it really didn't matter if he wasn't there anyway, since the new girl, Largo, with the signature wet hair couldn't understand a word of English ... or any other language perhaps. But in thinking about the phone booth, Rad remembered a conversation with Moe, about hot-wiring phone booths ... you know ... at first, the idea was to make a few free calls ... and then later ... for joy rides. Just something Moe did as a kid.

Moe had casually noted that the reason you don't see many phone booths around any longer is that all the smart people have flown off into space in them.

Rad thought about that.

"Well, Moe, what does that say about us?"

Moe thought about that in return.

"Guess it means we're running out of time, Rad."

In the retrospective pump head, a thought was beginning to glow like a lava lamp warming up. Rad could shut off the water to the hydrant. And then Moe could fix the ship. The Planet X ship. If he could make a phone booth fly, he could get this thing back in the air. Moe could even follow along in a phone booth on the way to intergalactic Shangri-La.

Oh, wait. Somebody had to know where to go.

And what about running out of time? That must have been an expression, right? How can you run out of something that is spherical in nature? [44]

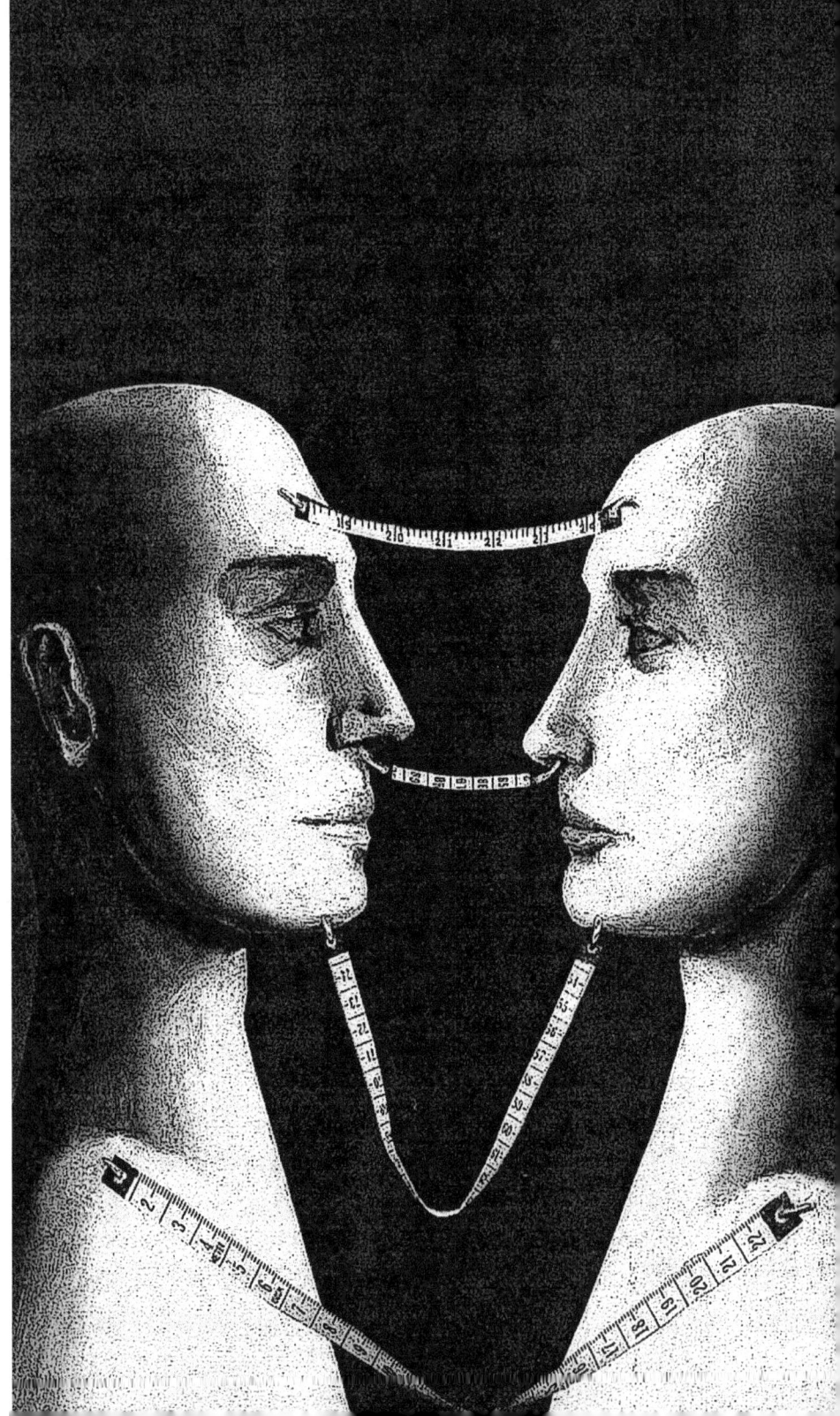

CHAPTER 20

The soldiers on the corner
regard us with evil eye,
barrels shimmering in burning sun,
street hot enough to melt soles.
The soldiers on the corner
Look at us with evil eye.

Shadow man in the shade
Thinks he's got it made.
But that's not his shadow:
It's another with a blade.
Oh, the poor bastard
He's been made.

The soldiers on the corner
Look at us with evil eye
Isn't that the sun crossing the sky?
I can't find my papers.
I wonder why
We all have to die?

[45] TRPB 611.905.2266
Very psychedelic, underground
comic book, *circa* 1970, loosely
based on surfers seeking the
magical "eye of god" inside
the rolled-over wave (tube).

[46] TRPB 611.905.2266
Another underground
comic book.

[47] TRPB 611.905.2266
Hf — a shiny metal used in the
reactor control rods of nuclear
power plants (probably because
it really does have the capacity
to absorb neutrons).

[48] TRPB 611.905.2266
Hafnia was the Roman name
for Copenhagen.

The garage doors were open, and the pumps had been turned on. Moe was in his workshop, looking at a very smallish bit of metal under a microscope. He was listening to something through headphones as well.

Rad didn't want to disturb the mechanic, who looked uncharacteristically perplexed. So he sat down and started leafing through some books on the little crowded coffee table. Most of the books were too thick to be of interest. For a guy who often said "if it takes you 300 pages to explain something, you don't know what you are talking about," Moe sure had a lot of thick books. This one had 787 pages on metallurgy. And here was one with 1690 pages on something that wasn't even in English. But there was some good stuff, too: there was a *Flaming Carrot Head* comic book and one called *Tales from the Tube.*[45] Rad opted for *Tales from the Tube* since it had better colours and *Zap #6* [46] wasn't there any more.

Rad had just gotten to the a section about damning up the Bay of Fundy for the ride of a lifetime and a certain glimpse into the eye of god, when Moe took off his headphones and shook his head: sideways, which he often did — as opposed to up-and-down, which is what The Pump Boy usually did.

"What's the matter, Moe?" Rad said quietly.

"I think this is hafnium," Moe said, tapping at the little piece of metal under the microscope.

Rad could hear the faint strains of music escaping out of the headphones. It sounded like an organ fugue, but Rad didn't recognise it — odd that, since he was a bit of an organ fan. It was largo and unusual. It sounded like an old instrument: like an early organ with a slow response, back before the pneumatic actions of the 1830s. Anyway, it seemed rude to ask two questions at once.

"At first I thought it was zirconium," Moe said, still tapping at the sample, "but ... it's hafnium, all right." [47]

"Are they similar?"

"Yes and no. They look the same but have very different melting points. You're looking at over 2200 degrees here — Centigrade. That's the high one."

"Wow. That's a lot. Is hafnium a Danish import?" [48]

"I think that's where it was discovered. But this piece didn't come from Denmark. I don't know where this came from," Moe said, "This bit may have come from Mars, for all I know. Or maybe some place even farther away."

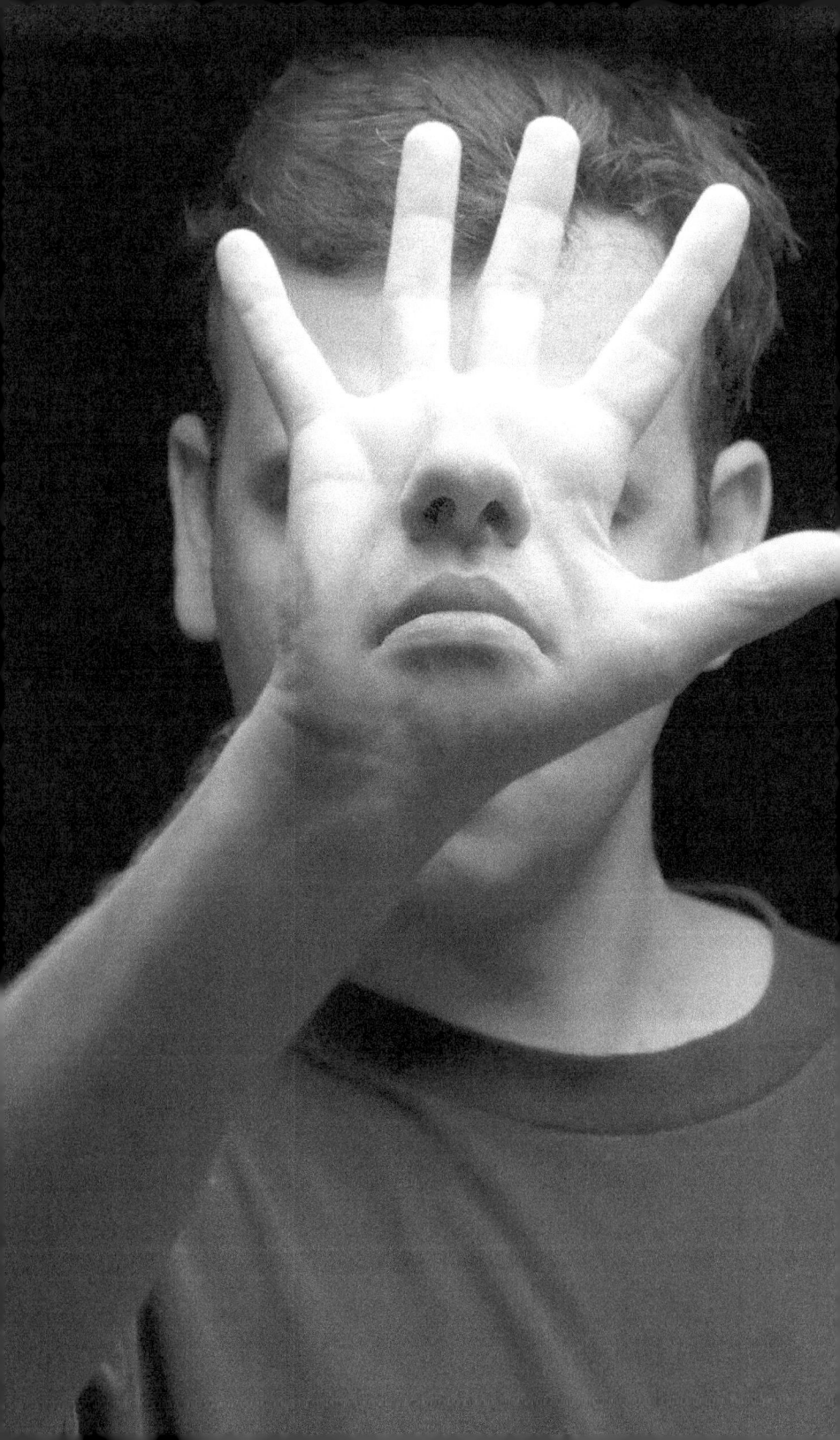

The Pump Boy sensed something different in Moe, something almost sorrowful. And that practically never happened — or never had.

"Moe, is there something broken that you can't fix?"

"Nah!" Moe said, pushing his wheeled chair away from the workbench and spinning it around en route to Rad, "Heck! I can fix it. But I'm gonna need your help. And maybe a little homework on neutrons."

"Gosh, Moe, the only thing that I have ever worked on other than the Rambler is a time machine. And, you know, it was the old-fashioned type that was kind of like a cart with lots of whirligigs and cranks on it. Some guy brought it into the shop. I told him I didn't usually fix stuff like that. I do instru-ments, on and off. You know."

"What was wrong with the time machine?"

"It didn't work. Maybe a problem with the neutrons, huh?"

Moe stuck an unlit cigar in his mouth and wheeled his chair back to the workbench.

"Had it ever worked?" he asked through clenched teeth.

Rad shrugged the padded shoulders. "I guess that it must have worked once"

"How ya figure?"

"Well," The Pump Boy said, while fooling with his tie, "It got here, didn't it?"

Moe's head started shaking from side to side again, only not as much: "This belongs to a friend of yours," Moe said, tapping at the metallic sample again. "Look, Rad, umm ... I have a complicated situation going on."

"Well, sure Moe, everything is complicated. Just ask Hammering Jim."

"Jim makes things complicated, Rad. I'm talking about something a little more complicated than even he could invent, something that was already complicated."

"Oh, like the stuff about mirrors, aliens, spherical time, and neutrons? That kind of complicated?"

Moe lit his cigar, took a few puffs, and stared at The Pump Boy through a blue cloud. Moe's head bobbed up and down agreeably in the cloud. That always made Rad feel better — he knew that if the head bobbed sideways that it would tip over the robot in the brain and cause confusion. This was a fact that anyone could observe just by paying a little attention.

"Yeah," Moe said, "that kind of complicated."

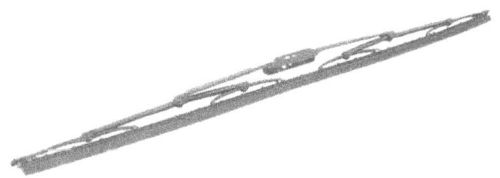

on again
off again
just tell me when

KillFlash knew darn well that it was against the law to park on the sidewalk. And there was the matter of shearing off a hydrant, leaving the scene of an accident, unregistered vehicle, and let's see ... what else? No windshield wiper. Normally, he wouldn't be in the sector, but there had been a complaint a week or so ago about the water, so he knew he had to show up sooner or later. And his preference was later. Since there really wasn't anything he could do about the water, he decided to write a ticket.

After citing as many violations as he could recall, he was now burdened with the problem of finding a place to leave the ticket, since, as noted, there were no windshield wipers. As he thought about this, the accidental fountain continued to pelt him with rain.

"Well, if this isn't screwed up," he mumbled rhetorically. And then, quickly concluding that thinking over the situation wasn't likely to provide a solution, he left the mini-rainstorm, tore up the ticket, and continued with the mumbling: "They would have gotten off anyway — aliens have a way of doing that. Besides, it's my break time. The Slip opens at noon, and maybe someone in that foreign planet crew knows something about this thing, anyway."

It was only a few blocks.

Larry's was unusually quiet — even for noon. There were no illegal and fractional foreign-planet types with bad ties. They probably hadn't even gotten up yet. That's just the way they were. Of course, there is a time zone difference, so I guess you had to allow for that.

"How about a beer, Larry?"

"You on duty, Flash?"

"Not right now, I'm not."

Larry shuffled over to the taps and tried one or two until he got one that worked.

"Here ya go, Flash. So ... what's it, raining out?"

"No," KillFlash said. "A nice day with low haze and kind of medium grey. No wind. Warm, of course, but not so bad."

Larry just stood there — watching the water drip off the uniform onto the floor, gathering in a small, potentially slippery puddle.

"You're all wet, KillFlash."

"Oh, that. That's nothing. I was writing up a ticket under a busted hydrant. Kind of a localised weather event, ya might say. I think some alien ditched a spacecraft over in the sector. Thought I might find someone in here that knows something."

Larry put his hands on the bar in front of KillFlash and leaned slowly into the KillFlash personal space: "Well, I seriously doubt that," he said.

"But I've seen 'em in here," KillFlash warned.

"People who know something?"

"No, you know: aliens, Larry."

"Really? Well, I haven't," Larry said, backing away from the bar and adjusting his personalised toque for added authority. "I don't see so great, ya know, especially with all the smoke. But I'll be sure to let you know if I hear anything, or run into anybody who knows anything."

Just then there was a bit of a racket outside: a noisy engine making whoosh-whoosh sounds, accompanied by burping chirps of tyres pawing at the pavement. And then silence. And then the ka-thump-thump of two car doors.

"That would be the Rad Boy and Moe the mechanic. Must be out for lunch," Larry said, just as the door swung open, spilling the two hafnium experts into the Limited Slip.

KillFlash didn't look up. Moe was a good mechanic — when he worked. But KillFlash had dropped a car off months ago. It was disturbing. And The Pump Boy wasn't any better. His brother-in-law's trombone had been in Rad's musical instrument repair shop for almost a year. Can't anyone do his job any more?

Well, Moe had a tough childhood, they said, and there were plenty of rumours. Moe had been in a little trouble with the law as a kid, which, well, wasn't that long ago. Nothing big: hot-wiring a few cars and phone booths, usually returning them after a night on the road — or in the sky. And Moe was known for hanging out with unusual if not downright exotic characters. KillFlash looked at The Pump Boy, noting that he was not in uniform, but was wearing multi-coloured sneakers, another tie that had been cut in half, and hair that looked like a frightened porcupine. Case in point, he thought.

Maybe it was time to get back on the shift, anyway. He could always ask these guys for

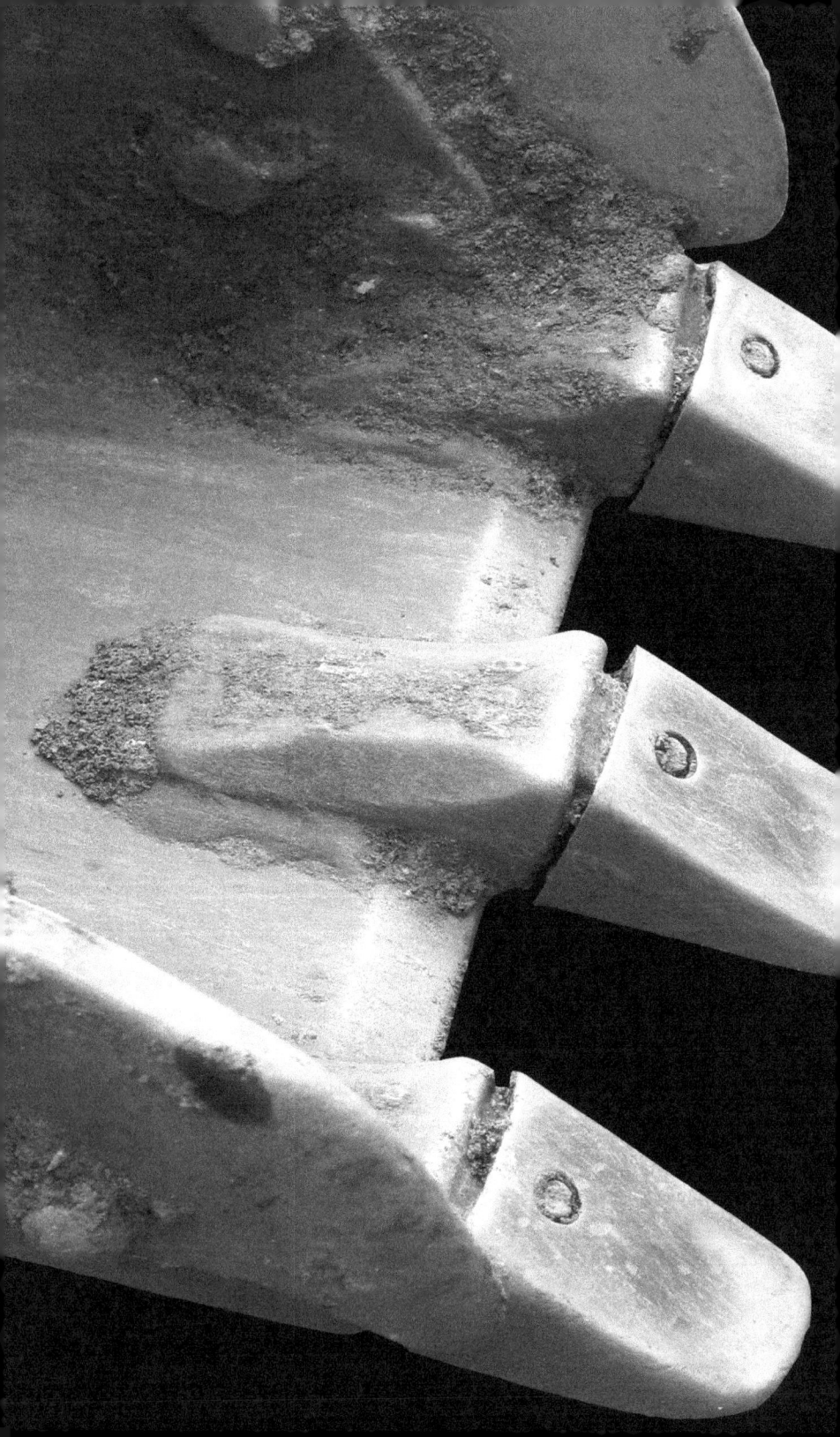

an update later…and maybe even mention the hydrant to The Pump Boy. He did work for the Known Water Authority, after all. Nah, not today. Maybe another time.

"Hey, thanks for the beer, Larry. Gotta run, but I'll be back about this. I'll be back all right."

KillFlash passed Moe and Rad, nodding a polite recognition.

"Parts are on order," Moe said, eliciting a glance from KillFlash. "They don't make the parts any more. Hard to get parts for any American car, especially transmission parts. So I have to work with a salvage yard. Grave diggers. I think that there are more cars stacked up in the yards than there are on the roads, ya know?"

"I know," KillFlash said, "It's a problem. Why, I don't even have a police car."

Everyone stood still for a moment. KillFlash was still dripping on the floor, and Moe and Rad were waiting for their eyes to adjust to the near lightless Limited Slip.

"Times are tough," noted The Pump Boy.

* * *

There wasn't any more to say.

Rad had certainly summed things up neatly. So KillFlash went back on patrol, and Moe and The Pump Boy enjoyed some french fries and beers. Moe was busy with some calculations on a napkin, and Rad was playing a game of tic-tac-toe against himself. Everything was going really well.

"So what are you two doing with yourselves today? Other than the obvious?" Larry said as he refilled the glasses.

"Oh, fixin' stuff," Rad said, closing in on victory and making a final X — or was he O?

"Yeah," Larry said. "So I heard."

Moe looked up from his calculations. "What the hell are you talkin' about, Larry? Where did you hear something like that?"

Rad wondered whether the going-really-well party was about to come to an abrupt halt. Moe's brain robot was now awake and was in a bad mood.

"Well, you just told Flash that you were getting his old cruiser ready to roll. That's fixing something, isn't it?"

"Oh … yeah," Moe said, rapidly returning to normal. "That. Yeah, I'm getting that fixed, all right."

Rad wondered.

**most of the living world,
is below the surface of the sea,
invisible to us,
and most serene.**

**and above the oceans,
in the thin, fragile host of air,
uncountable insects hum,
it's not our scene.**

**though we have never been,
to the centre of the Earth
so much deeper than the sea:
how smart we seem.** [49]

Rad almost lost his way en route to the shop. It was upsetting when the Rambler forgot where it was going.

Deep down inside, he knew that it was partly his fault. Not sure which part, of course. But, then again, the concept of "fault" was hard to figure out. Maybe no one ever did — or ever would. It was something that was very important to Jim and Fuzzy, but meaningless to Moe, Larry, and, he suspected, Largo Lips. So who was right?

All of them?

None of them?

"None of the above," he said to himself. That had always been his favourite answer in school. Who could doubt the certainty of uncertainty? Other than the teachers? They didn't know what was true, of course, they just thought that they did.

Rad had never gotten on well in school. It was such a crazy place. Good for doodling, of course.

To be practical about observations, let's note that Moe and Largo Lips seemed to be in good moods most of the time, and Larry, too, now that he had gotten to know him (though you had to watch what you said about ... you know ... aliens). And whose fault was that?

The Radical Pump Boy (shrugging) decided rather rapidly that the whole concept of fault was too confusing, too easily manipulated, to be of further interest. He merely stabbed at the gas pedal and sniffed old-car smell. Life was a cool place to hang out.

But sure enough, the shop was where it had always been — at the very bottom of an enormous building, constructed in what was considered "Gothic style," according to Jim, or had that been Moe, or had it been someone else? Everyone was someone else anyway, so maybe it didn't really matter.

Nobody lived or worked or even hung out in the top part. Not any more. Maybe that added to the Gothic elements, which were vaguely Egyptian looking[50] at least to Rad. Egyptians were cool, weren't they? Rad often wondered what people used to do here, in the many floors above, in the funny, funky times gone by.

What had they done?
Why had they left?
Where did they go?
Who was to know?

Someday these mysteries, and the many other questions stored in the Rad head, would be answered — of this he was very confident, though not certain. *Certainty* was a notion reserved for the exclusive use of the totally insane — and teachers, of course.

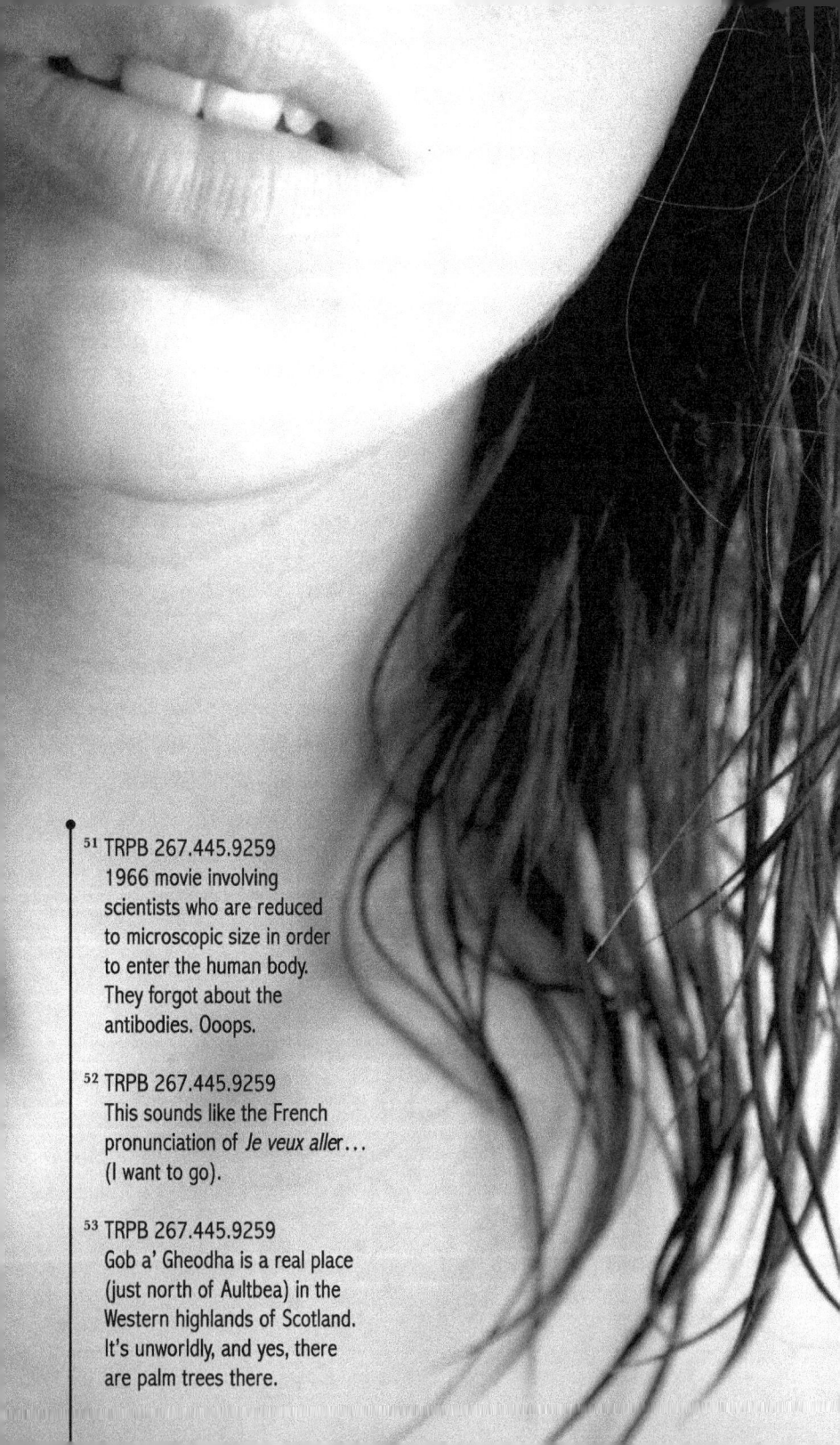

[51] TRPB 267.445.9259
1966 movie involving
scientists who are reduced
to microscopic size in order
to enter the human body.
They forgot about the
antibodies. Ooops.

[52] TRPB 267.445.9259
This sounds like the French
pronunciation of *Je veux aller*...
(I want to go).

[53] TRPB 267.445.9259
Gob a' Gheodha is a real place
(just north of Aultbea) in the
Western highlands of Scotland.
It's unworldly, and yes, there
are palm trees there.

Well, *probably*, let's say.

He made his way carefully through the basement, avoiding both glowing puddles and hissing pipes and dodging droplets of day-glo colours. It would be easy to imagine the basement as being alive and walking through it as a sort of tour of an organism like those guys in *Fantastic Voyage*[51] cruising around inside somebody else's body. That's just the kind of place the basement was.

The walk was short, which was a good thing.

It was nice to enter the shiny and well-decorated shop. So familiar — even though it looked as though everything had been rearranged. And there was Largo Lips polishing instruments. They all looked so lovely, while she looked so content. Largo looked up and said something incomprehensible about Juvus Alley,[52] nodding at the ceiling again, but Rad didn't even know where that alley was because most of the street signs had disappeared years ago. Rad wondered where on Earth — or somewhere else — they could have gone?

There was, Rad started to think, something very attractive about her hair. It was so seldom that you saw girls with wet hair. Oh well, lots of work to do. Maybe today would be a good day for the trombone.

As the Pump Boy walked past Largo Lips, he noted that she had tacked a very sharp photograph to the half wall just in front of her hangout place. It seemed to glow like a little television tube — remember what slides looked like back in the old days?

But it was such a little photo.

It was a photograph of a beach or a bay — there were rocks, and palm trees, and dense white clouds sleeping over their shadows. For all the world it looked like the Mountains of the Moon ... or Gob a' Gheodha ... right out of Aultbea[53] ... or maybe, maybe, Shangri-La. But like life, it looked like a cool place to hang out.

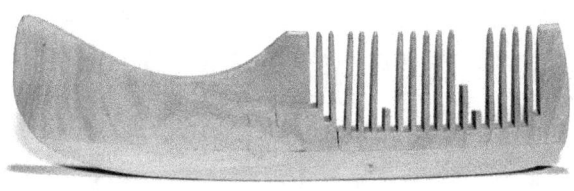

CHAPTER 23

**When water used to run,
we all had fun.
Now,
it's all undone.
Some think it's funny
And some think none.**

Moe had never left Larry's Limited Slip (It's differential!). He had more calculations to do. What with dark energy and other bothersome concepts, it was pretty easy to use up a whole napkin — especially a cocktail napkin.

Even two of them.

"Here," Larry said, tossing down a handful of little paper squares, "Have at it, Moe."

"Thanks, Larry."

"So, can you fix that ship?"

Moe kept calculating. There was a crinkling cellophane sound and the cha-chink, flip, cha-chink, click of Moe's cigarette lighter. But no words until the ATR Moe had exhaled:

"What do you mean, Larry?"

"Come on, Moe, that brunette who came in to see you last night. She gave you some parts: little metallic parts, right? She doesn't speak a word of English."

"Her car broke down, Larry. I'm a mechanic. How about a bag of chips?"

Larry lifted a little gate and wandered around to the customer side of the bar. He was wiping the bar clean and then sneaker-squeaking in the old KillFlash drip area. He slowly and squeakingly made his way down to Moe's bar stool.

Chirp, chirp ... Squeak. Chirp.

54 TRPB 535.115.4000
All references to unusual sci-fi
movies from 1959 to 1984. *Plan 9
from Outer Space* – maybe the
worst sci-fi movie ever made.
The 8th dimension comes from the
1984 *Adventures of Buckaroo
Bonzai* – much better. Because
it has been concluded that most of
everything that we know is 99.995%
empty space, we should be able to
pass right through it. Entire worlds
could coexist with our own.

55 TRPB 298.122.4237
Probably Eigen decomposition
equations, boiled down from a
square matrix – used in physics,
possibly being used for stability
analysis.

"I won't say anything, Moe, honest," Larry whispered (chirp). "I know what you are really fixing. And I won't tell anyone. These are my best customers. Just as they are yours. We all know that, don't we? Oh maybe some come from Plan 9 ... and some from Planet of Blood ... and others from the 8th dimension [54] ... what does it really matter? I don't care what they do on their own time. It's none of my business. And most of them don't worry about what I do either."

Moe kept scribbling away with eigenvector decomposition equations [55] — at least, that's what they looked like.

"Thanks, Larry, I know this is a good club. You know my friends. I'm just trying to make a living, just like you. And if I can help somebody along the way ... all the better."

"Especially," Larry said, halting the squeaking sneakers, "if she's real ... real pretty?"

Moe looked up: "I wouldn't know anything about that, Larry. I'm a bachelor. She works for Rad. And Rad is my friend. If he likes someone, there's always a reason for it."

"So why haven't you told the boy about your project?"

"I'm not sure. He's vaguely aware of what's going on. But you know how it is with the Pumper: no matter what you say, he hears something else."

"Don't we all, Moe?"

"I guess."

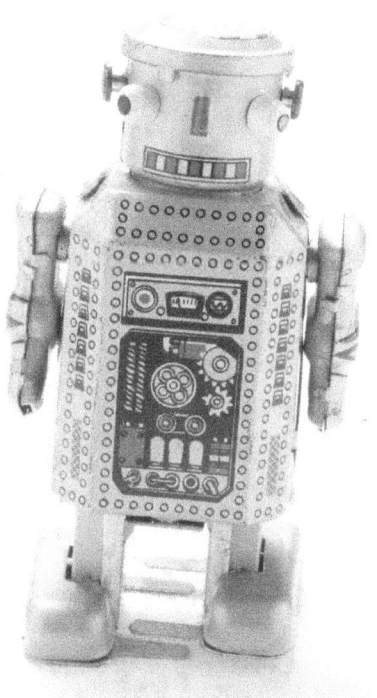

⁵⁶ TRPB 421.006.8998
Another reference *to Orpheus,* Jean Cocteau's
use of a mirror as a passage to the underworld,
and between this world and the next world, and
of course, a reference to *Through the Looking
Glass (And What Alice Found There).* In either
case, mirrors are seen as a portal to the unseen,
even though they appear to reflect what can
be seen.

⁵⁷ TRPB 205.993.6974
"It's the illusion of being elsewhere."

**Those ever-loving eyes,
bigger than lies.
Science is never nice.
White mice on a table.
Very few are able
to dance
and tell me a fable.**

Molecules were everywhere. They made it hard to concentrate.

Reflection in the polished brass. A kaleidoscopic view of a world of unknown size, impossible to measure, impossible to be sure. Only possible to imagine. Isn't that where everything is anyway?

He could see himself oblong and oozing, now. Now skinny and long, his cheek sliding down the side of the trombone. Was this what things really looked like?

She had done this. She had polished the trombone. She had polished everything.

She would make a mirror out of anything if she could.

Why?

Don't all mirrors lie?

Except the kind that you can walk through.

So were these the kind that you could walk through? [56]

The Pump Boy stood up and walked on a rubber floor. He could see Largo Lips in the front of the shop, polishing the keys on a bassoon. There's something defective in the human brain, isn't there? Something that keeps us wanting things because we think that we do and there's no other reason. How did thoughts end up being reasons?

Is it all because so much of what we say has nothing to do with an effective reality? And so much of what we think is about a future that is wholly imagined — isn't it?

Why do we say these things?

Behaviour models like the carrot and the stick. Why don't people realise that the carrot is really the stick and the stick is really the carrot?

Rad had been talking to Largo Lips the whole time. She just smiled at him and shrugged her shoulders with a somewhat Rad-like philosophical abandon — that's what he would have called it, anyway. Or had he?

"*C'est l'illusion d'être ailleurs,*" [57] she said.

[58] TRPB 651.914.9244
Basically, same as "There's
no place like home." This
may have a connection with
The Wizard of Oz.

Rad nodded, since that seemed the polite thing to do. He had the feeling that whatever she had said must have made sense, somewhere.

Plus it sounded cool. Largo rocked her head a little as she spoke, as people do when they are talking to themselves.

There was something pleasant about not being able to understand someone, especially if it didn't seem to matter. And it never mattered as much as people thought it did, anyway. For want of a better word, it seemed ever so *realistic* for words to make no sense. It was better than thinking that you understood, or were understood — either of which people believe is possible. But how could it be? Things are barely rather than fully understood. It's the great joke of the brain robots. Every head hears the same sentence in a different way. Every speaker thinks that he's making sense. Like looking in a mirror, what you think is there has nothing to do with what's really there — since ... nothing is.

It was too mind-boggling to contemplate any further.

"What a crazy world it is," Rad said.

smiling at the expert instrument polisher.

Largo Lips smiled back at him and then put one of her two-toned fingernails on the little glowing picture of the beach somewhere near Gob a' Gheodha. She rapped on the picture ever so slightly, which caused it to move. As if your head were turning at the beach. That was cool.

"*On n'est vraiment bien que chez soi,*" [58] she said.

Rad nodded in agreement, having absolutely no idea what the beautiful woman with the damp hair was saying.

But she had to have been right. You could tell.

"I want to go there," Rad said, as he watched the changing camera angles.

She looked at the ceiling again, as she often did when talking unintelligibly, and pointed at it in a very knowing way.

Rad suddenly had the strangest feeling. It was time to leave the shop. It was his shift at the Known Water Authority, and he had to go home, find his uniform, and arrive sometime at the KWA. There was no point in holding things up and standing there feeling strange. But of all the odd thoughts, he felt a desire to touch Largo Lips, to smell her hair.

DIESEL

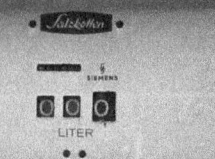

LITER

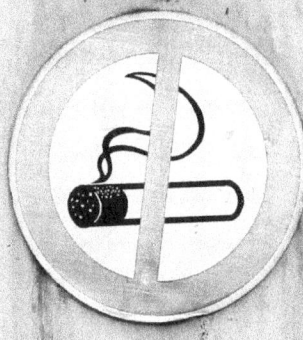

Rauchen verboten
Motor und Fremdheizung abstellen
Abgabe nur in geeignete Gefäße

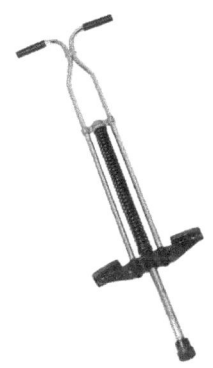

CHAPTER 25

Going up here
Coming down there
This is what we do
At the pogo fair

The Pump Boy stepped over the usual collection of minor rubble as he approached the gates to the KWA. There sure wasn't much respect for buildings anymore, and as buildings went, this was a pretty cool looking one. A long time ago, this one had been an armoury. Maybe they made armour in it. Maybe there were knights and daze and strange women lying about in ponds.

But now, there were workers staring at old computer screens, and there were valves and pipes, and just as many leaks.

The Rad desk (which had his name on it) was piled high with paperwork that no one had bothered to throw out. He started collecting handfuls for just such an exercise when he noticed several complaint forms about a broken fire hydrant.

He knew that hydrant.

KillFlash knew about it, too.

And maybe Moe.

The Pump Boy didn't like the idea of disturbing one of the computer people, but it seemed pretty clear that something had to be done. They had to figure out how to shut off the water to that hydrant, and then, someday, maybe replace it.

Bart was at his terminal and even seemed to be awake. Let's start there.

"Say Bart," Rad said, handing one of the complaint forms to glowing face, "I have a problem here, and I bet you can help me figure it out. Can we get a crew to shut this hydrant off? We're losing a lot of water over there. Can you handle this for me?"

[59] TRPB 611.905.2266
Taken from the classic
response from the lead
character in Melville's *Bartleby
the Scrivener*, who responded
to all of his boss's requests
with "I'd prefer not to." Even
when fired for doing nothing,
Bartleby still came to the office
and did nothing.

Bart leaned back in his chair and spent a long time reading over the sentence-long complaint.

"I don't know," he said, placing the form neatly on a stack of very similar-looking papers, "I'd prefer not to." [59]

Bart had been with the KWA for a long time. Maybe he was tired. Maybe there was someone else. Maybe Rad would just have to do it himself: he had a toolbox (it was yellow and black) and he knew where the hydrant was.

"Thanks anyway, Bart. I'm going out there this afternoon. I'll take a look at it myself."

"Suit yourself, Rad. If you don't make it back, can I have that lava lamp?"

* * *

As the Pump Boy was loading his toolbox in the Rambler, he thought about maybe asking Moe to come along. Moe was good with mechanical stuff. And tools usually ended up doing mechanical things. Usually, but not always. There had been times when tools, Rad's tools, had been used for music. The ratchet, in particular, had been very useful, with its cha-chuur cha-churr rhythm particularly effective on top of the bong bwong of the saw. And some of the wrenches had such a pleasant ting.

Ah yes, those were the good old days: sitting around jamming with your friends, making music out of nuts and bolts that had nothing else to do.

Rad made a hand signal and pulled away from the curb.

There were a lot of hungry cars at Moe's place, but no Moe.

Rad started shuffling around pumping gas left and right. All the cars were in a good mood, most of them purring, and whoosh-whooshing delightedly, and one of the skateboard cars, like Moe's, rumbling. Many of the Moe cars that came to drink at the station had turbochargers, which, as handy as they might be, kind of ruined the cool sound of the engine by taking the beat out of it. It wasn't the same. You couldn't hear the pulse, which made the cars seem less alive.

Moe's new paint job involving the tropical colours was a big hit.

The cars drank up and darted off, looking something like a pack of wheeled wolves.

[60] TRPB 165.355.4163
Note, some music scholars believe
that it is incorrect to refer to a
fugue as a piece of music, for it
is really the form of composition
rather than the result.

[61] TRPB 165.355.4163
These descriptions refer to actual
parts of a pipe organ and how
they are employed, which seems
to point to couplers from the
mid-1800s.

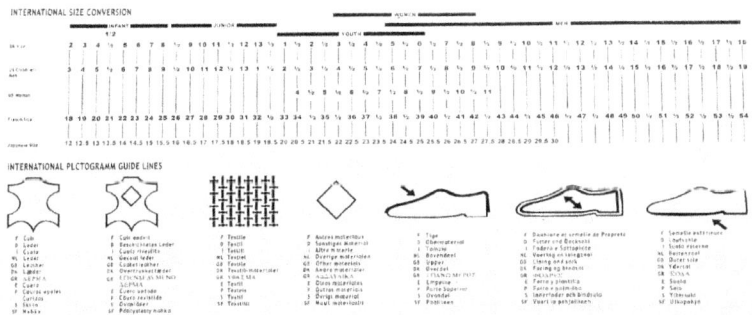

Rad wandered into the shop and looked around again for Moe, but there was no Moe. The light was still on at the workbench, and the little bits of shiny metal were there — and Moe's headphones, and what looked like some kind of a recording device, but not like the usual kind. It was also very shiny, but probably not hafnium.

It was hard to resist a new kind of toy.

The pump head adorned itself with the headphones and started fooling around with the shiny little device

Nothing much happened at first, but suddenly the headphones produced the sound of organ music written in fugue — or at least that seemed to be where it was going. [60]

The parts started their journey: developed and contrasted in G minor, or at least something rather close. The Pump Boy could not identify the composer, the composition, or even the era. But based on the speed that attached the Swell, the organ itself must have been an old one with Sforzando couplers. [61]

"Man," Rad said, "Moe is funky after all. Beat poet, master mechanic, and an organ head into unknown music. That's cool."

Maybe it wasn't polite to listen to someone else's unknown music for organ heads? What if he couldn't turn this thing off? Rad looked at the shiny little music box and saw his face — at least a version of it — looking back at him. There was only one button on the little box, and that was the one that he had used to start the music. So he pushed it again.

Silence. Whew! That was close.

Well, Moe or no Moe, the hydrant had to be stopped.

The Pump Boy wandered out to the Rambler, wiped a few droplets of sky gunk off the windshield, and headed for the hydrant geyser and spaceship wreckage.

[62] TRPB 535.115.4000
This is the exact phrase from the book
Alice's Adventures in Wonderland, with the
only change being man-hole in the place of
rabbit-hole. It describes Alice's first steps
into Wonderland (Underground).

CHAPTER 26

Right for tight
and left for loose.
Tonight's the night
to cook the goose.

Nothing had changed at the crash site. Same giant crêpe pan with portholes along the top. Plenty of colour within the rain area. The big change was understanding why it was raining, which seemed pretty obvious now. But that always happens when you figure something out? Well, not always: sometimes it even makes it worse.

Rad parked on the edge of the rainstorm and disappeared into a nearby manhole that was missing its cover. A brightly coloured sawhorse guarded the man-hole. On it, the words "NO COVER" had been painted.

It wasn't raining under the street, but it was like a shrunken version of the basement leading to the shop. Lots of pipes and drips and hisses. Very little light. Rad had never been down a man-hole, but he had heard about what could happen in rabbit-holes and knew that the opposite of everything happened in black holes. Didn't it?

The man-hole went straight on like a tunnel for some way, and then dipped suddenly down,[62] so suddenly that it caused the Pump Boy's hair quills to stand up even straighter than usual!

"All this is a little too familiar," he said, followed by, "Cool. A waterfall. Neat paint job."

An overhead grid had cut the light from the sky into diagonal stripes that brushed across a damp floor and hissing pipes and valves. Water was pouring into the side of the grid and rippling away in the diagonal sunlight.

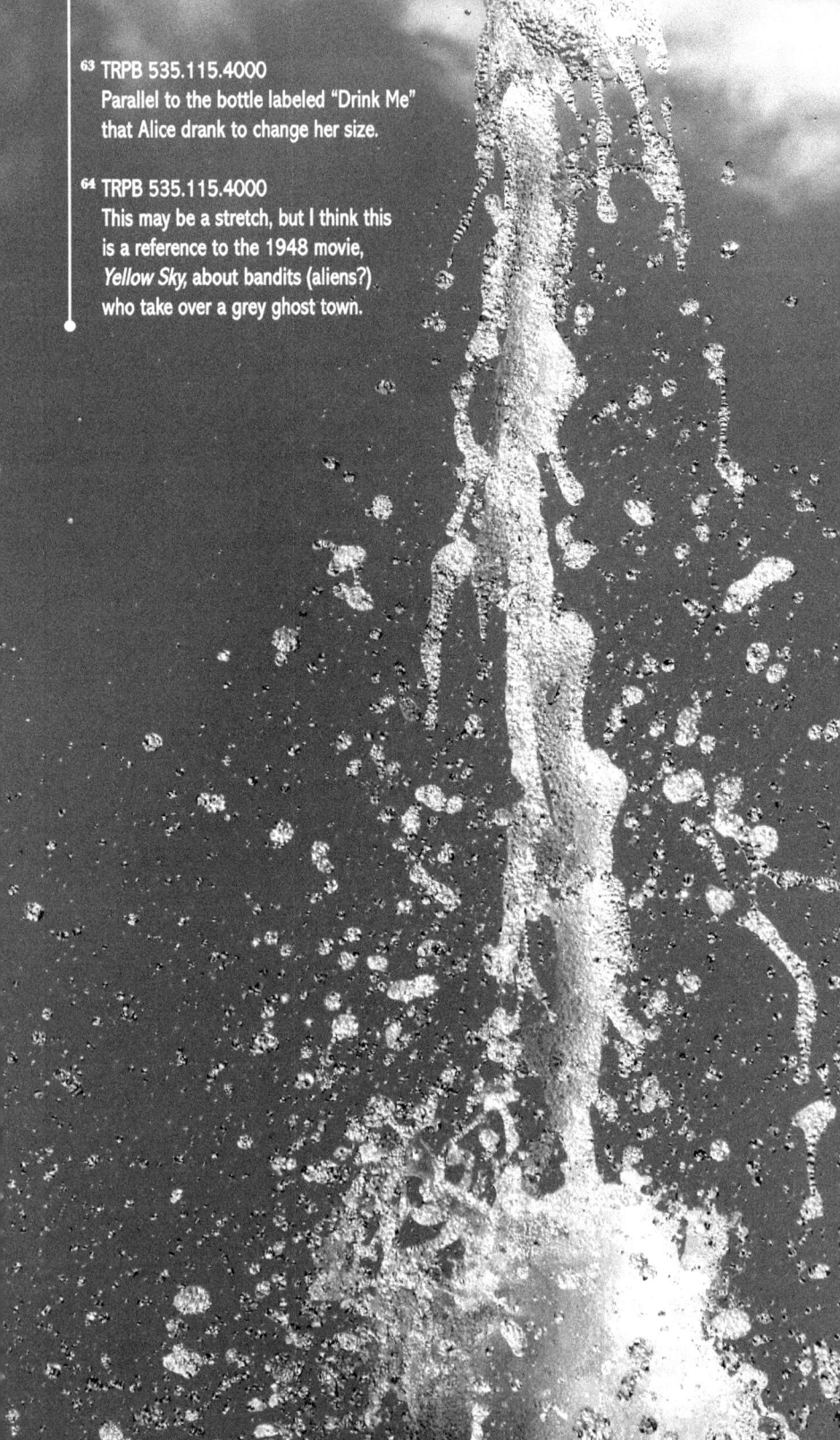

⁶³ TRPB 535.115.4000
Parallel to the bottle labeled "Drink Me"
that Alice drank to change her size.

⁶⁴ TRPB 535.115.4000
This may be a stretch, but I think this
is a reference to the 1948 movie,
Yellow Sky, about bandits (aliens?)
who take over a grey ghost town.

"We must be under the rainstorm. I have a job to do," reminded The Pump Boy, supervisor at the Known Water Authority. There were plenty of valves and levers. It could have been confusing, but as luck would have it, dangling from one of the big valves was a large tag reading "TURN ME." [63]

Who knows what would happen now? Time to find out.

As Rad cranked away at the rusty valve, creating even greater eek-eek sounds than those from his sink at home, the waterfall began to fade away. Now the tunnel was almost silent, just the remaining hisses and invisible hum. Rad felt bad about the waterfall. But that's just way things go sometimes, or given enough time, always. Even the sphere of time eventually turns itself inside out. The hairs were standing up again: this was a very poor subject to contemplate in a man-hole. Time to get outta here.

The world above appeared to be unchanged. The Rambler was still there, and the spacecraft was sitting quietly in its little world of colour. All else was ghost town grey under the glowing yellow sky. [64]

Rad had gotten used to the giant crêpe pan. The *Man From Planet X* worries were fading —maybe it didn't matter what had happened in the movie. Unless you were in it.

Had he been in it?

Anyway, what could be the harm in taking a peek inside? It was not very often that this opportunity for adventure came along.

Now that the rain had stopped, the expert finish on the craft was plainly visible: somebody really went wild with the chrome polish on this hot rod! Now it looked like a gigantic, highly polished, stainless steel crêpe pan. A little bit burned here and there — just like a regular crêpe pan. It had to have come from a very stylish planet.

It was silly to think that you know what's inside an alien spacecraft just because you have seen a few movies, after all. It all depends on what movies you see.

"Let's face it," Rad said, talking to himself for additional support, "it's human nature to remember the really super scary stuff and forget the happy stuff. Or is it the other way around?"

Rad concluded that it would probably depend upon your personality, and he hadn't figured his out yet.

"We're just stalling here," he said, "Come on, let's just go take a peek."

[65] TRPB 165.355.4163
Another slightly bastardized bit
of French meaning *Air-tight
Windows Incorporated.*

[66] TRPB 165.355.4163
An inside joke. Iconic French
cigarettes, Gauloises, come in a
blue package *(paquet d'bleues)*
and have long been considered a
symbol of the French Resistance.
Indeed, the color is famous, and I
believe such shades are broadly
used in Klein's work (French).

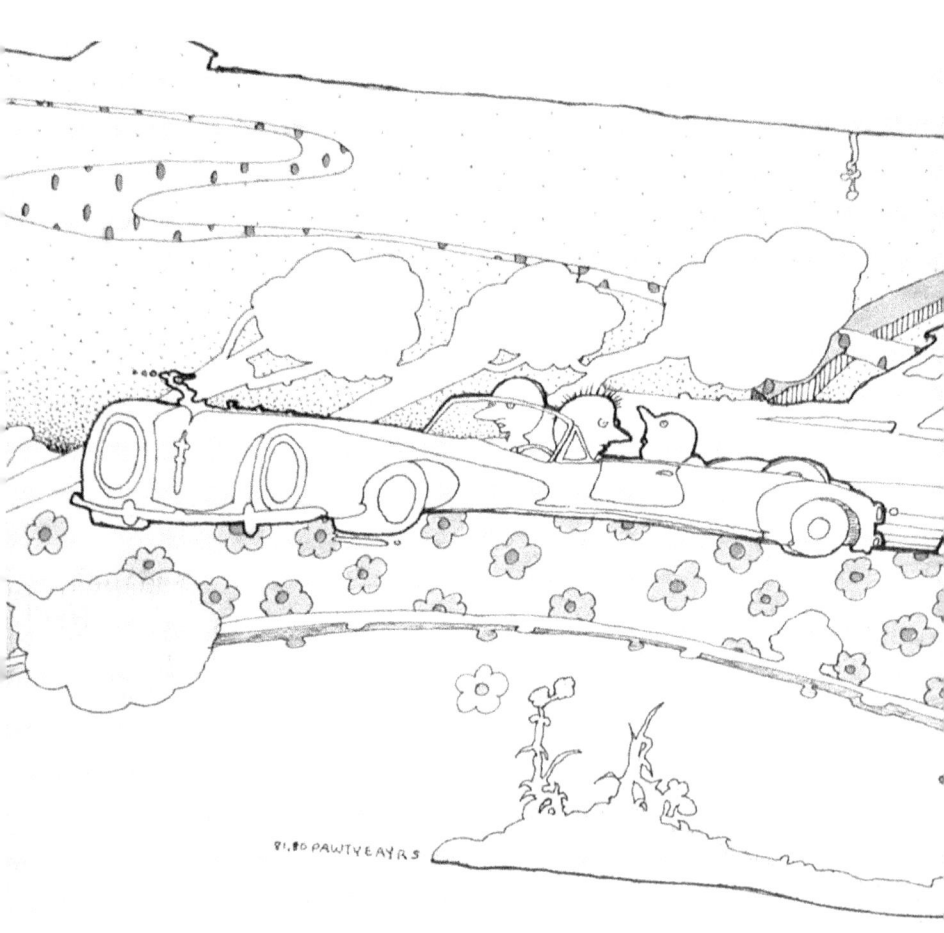

Inside

There was no hideous alien, overheated scuba-diving face in the window. Good. That would have cancelled the planned examination.

But the portholes — if that's what windows are called in a spaceship — were small. He was going to have to get within inches of one to see inside.

What was this?

Engraved in the frame of the porthole were the letters *Soc. Hublots Etanches* [65] — maybe it was the pilot's name — like you see on movie airplanes? Oh well, there was simply no way to know what these alien words meant.

The Pump Boy got even closer and looked just over the frame with the pilot's name on it and caught his first glance of the interior.

It looked a lot like the time machine that he had tried to fix, but very neat and very shiny — with what Rad imagined the interior of an upscale Victorian bar might have looked like. It was a cool look: lots of reflections, which is what is to be expected. And — looking all the way to one end, and then to the other — there were no aliens inside. Maybe they were out shopping. There was a dashboard up front, but no obvious sign of what kind of transmission might be employed.

Rad guessed automatic anyway.

Now get this: across from his window was a work station that looked a lot like the work station that Fuzzy had in the corner of her bathroom. At its centre, a big mirror, of course: you had to enter and leave the thing somehow. In front of that: the workbench with lots of bottles and jars. Bottles and jars and a pile of tools with unimaginable uses — just like Fuzzy's work station, for which she of course had a different name. There were the little golden tubes, too, and even an ashtray, next to which was a small, beautifully blue cigarette package [66] — looking like a dab out of an Yves Klein painting. There were also three picture frames on the vanity. The pictures were too far away to make out, and besides, one of the frames was empty.

Wait a minute.

Maybe there were aliens inside after all. What if they were invisible? They could be. Maybe their atoms were farther apart than ours? Who was looking at whom?

Okay, that will be quite enough of looking into Hublot's porthole for now. Time to find Moe and ask about getting this thing back on the road.

Rad was excited about what kind of sound it would make, and whether it would glow like Moe's gas island apron as it hovered a few inches off the ground.

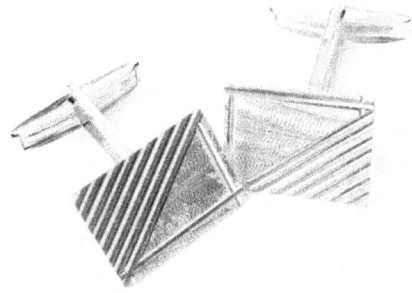

CHAPTER 27

Robin red breast
Raised in a shrinking nest
How was he to know
Where to go?

Rad thought it best to change into something more festive before heading over to the Limited Slip. He was feeling adventurous and excited about outer space. He found some socks with geometric patterns and one of those long-sleeved tee-shirts with the horizontal stripes. This would be a cool look. To make the best possible arrival, it would be necessary to drive the Rambler, and the Rambler should be fixed up as well.

The Pump Boy picked up a small brush and a can of black paint.

This would be cool.

But when he shook the can, there was no sloshing of paint inside, which is always a bad sign when it comes to cans of paint. Well, here was some red paint. It sloshed.

Rad took the paint outside and knelt down in front of the driver's door. On the centre of the door, he drew a picture of Saturn (always the coolest-looking planet). Then, above the picture of Saturn, he wrote COSMIC RANGER. The pump head nodded, "cool," then, below the picture of Saturn, he thought he should add a motto – if that's what those things are called.

This required quite a bit of thought. So he thought.

Finally, he wrote, in quotation marks, "Have head, will travel."

Perfect!

The Rambler should perhaps have a front sight as well, like Jim's car. Or, maybe not. If he had a robot head, that would be cool. But he didn't have a robot head. And besides, the spacecraft didn't have a sight on it.

So that left nothing to do but cruise over to Larry's for a drink and a little chat with Moe, beat poet, master mechanic, and an organ head into unknown music.

67 TRPB 651.914.9244
These are real cocktails, very old
school, but still to be found in
most bartending guides.

CHAPTER 28

So the sun leaves.
Away it goes,
Beyond the wires,
Into the trees.
Where it lands?
Nobody knows.

There was plenty of parking in front of The Limited Slip. But there was only one streetlight that was working, and though it was half a block away, this had to be the best place to show off the Rambler.

As Rad stepped away from the car, he noted that his painting could have been a little better: some of the COSMIC RANGER paint had run a bit, intersecting with the ring around Saturn. But the overall effect still looked official – and adventurous.

Inside, it was more like the usual Limited Slip. Moe was in the back with his alien pals, engulfed in a glittering smoky sphere. Larry was behind the bar lecturing to a few sleepy-eyed patrons. A few Fuzzies were at the end of the bar near the door to the water closets.

There was no table service at Larry's, so you had to go to the bar if you wanted a drink, some chips, or a bag of crisps. This would make it easy to get a word in with Moe. He'd have to come to the bar sooner or later – well, later obviously – since he always bought the beer and chips for his table.

Rad plopped himself down in front of the beer taps. Even though it was night time, pretty much, his eyes still had to adjust to the dark blue mirror light of Larry's Limited Slip.

"So what's it gonna be tonight?" Larry, the Mixicologist, finally inquired.

"Larry, I feel like a real drink tonight."

"That's good, because I'm down to just one beer on tap."

"What kind of drinks are space-related?"

Larry looked at The Pump Boy, put down his ever-present wipe-up rag, and lit a cigarette, "Space-related drinks?" he asked from under a long plume of smoke that just missed Rad's head.

"Yeah, with names that you find in outer space. Like Saturn or uh ... Cosmic."

"Well, Rad, I don't really know what you might find in outer space, having never gone there, myself. But I know what ya find in bars, having, basically, never left one. So how about some cocktail classics like the Star, the Eclipse, the Blue Moon, or the Skyrocket? I'm not sure about the Xanthia? Is that some kind of planet?" [67]

⁶⁸ TRPB 535.115.4000
Area in Asia Minor. There are
statues from the region
carved in what is now
called Xanthian marble.

⁶⁹ TRPB 535.115.4000
Unconventional, three-act film
(1996) about a bunch of
childish, would-be robbers
who, of all things, focus on
"planning" in their consistently
inept attempts to lead a
romanticized life of crime.

"Umm, no, that was here, but it's gone now — except for the statues.[68] I like the sound of the Skyrocket."

"Sure, one Skyrocket comin' up. Even have the Swedish punch."

As Larry was shaking the Skyrocket and Rad was imagining how one might throw a Swedish punch, ATR Moe bumped up against the bar.

"Hey, Rad. What it is?"

"What it is, Moe?"

"That's a cool shirt. You look like a new-age beatnik. You should be drinking coffee and dashing off some rhymes." Moe started playing bongo drums on the bar.

The Pump Boy dug the beat, closed his eyes, and let the lines flow:

"I'm drinking a Skyrocket.
It's gonna tighten me like a socket.
I'm off to the moon.
Keys to space in my pocket.
and it's gonna be…
real soon."

Moe continued drumming on the bar, taking the lead from the RPB:

" — Space is the place," he said,
"Where you're never too far
from a shooting star.
Space is the place…
for another race."

Larry strained the chilled amber Skyrocket into Rad's cocktail glass and squinted at Moe.

"Looks to me like this is the place for another race," Larry mumbled.

"It's your place, Larry," Moe said as he switched off the bongos. "How about a half-dozen beers before we run out?"

Larry shifted over to the taps and started filling some glasses.

"Moe," Rad said, "We have to talk about something. I … uh … found something cool out near my shop."

"Sure Rad. I have something that I want to bring up myself. But I have some business here tonight. Come on into the station first thing in the morning. And, meanwhile, enjoy your Bottle Rocket."

"It's a Skyrocket, Moe. *Bottle Rocket* is a classic crime drama. The Skyrocket is a classic cocktail."

"Rad, *Bottle Rocket* [69] was a comedy, a spoof."

"Well, I thought it was pretty serious stuff. Sometimes things just don't work out for people, even people who want to be criminals. I mean, look at some of our plans."

"Which plan?"

"The plan to talk about something tomorrow, for instance. Can we agree on meeting at noon? I have to go to my shop in the morning?"

"Noon works."

"You see. That's planning."

"Rad," Moe said, "easy on the Sky-rockets. Okay?"

"Just two, Moe."

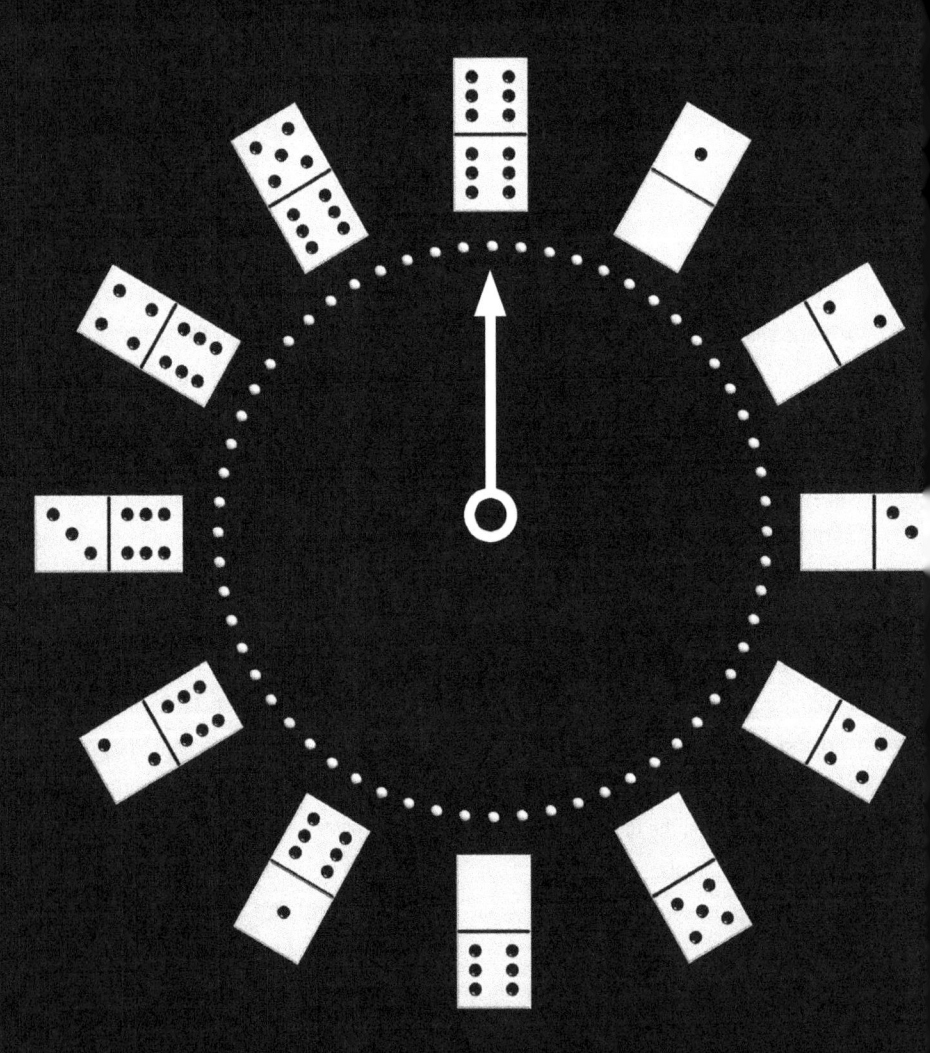

CHAPTER 29

HIGH NOON

How could anyone complain about getting up in the morning? Sure the pump head was pounding from the two Skyrockets — well, maybe it was the four Blue Moons that had been such a bright idea at the time. Maybe that was what you call a Swedish punch?

But at the very least, it was morning. A new day. What could be better?

"Would I rather repeat the best day of my life or have a whole new day?"

The answer seemed simple enough. There was something inherently wrong with trading a known for an unknown.

Rad had slept in the geometric-patterned socks and decided to wear them to the shop. He selected some multi-coloured sneakers to match, and a black vest. After adding some radical gel to keep the quill-like hairs standing surprisingly on end, he was into the official COSMIC RANGER patrol car, heading for the musical instrument repair shop. Head still pounding with that slow, vacant feeling of being empty.

"Cosmic Ranger. Have head, will travel," he said determinedly as he sent the patrol car into the street. It was such a perfect beginning: light grey glow of the forever day, and just enough mist to keep the scenery away.

Funny thing about days: how they don't add up. If you are 40 years old, you have lived almost 15,000 days, but you have no sense of 15,000 days. That would make you instantly insane, wouldn't it?

Rad shook off the thought. He was more interested in this day.

It's the only important day.

The old Citroën was parked in front of the shop. It must have just arrived, because it was not sleeping yet.

It was beautiful car with spaceship qualities. Rad looked inside at the comfortable seats and science-fiction-movie interior. There was a pamphlet on the passenger seat with a photograph of the Earth on it, but he couldn't understand the words.

Wait.

That was cool.

The image of the Earth on the pamphlet was not only glowing a little bit, but it was moving. Yes, the Earth was turning. It was

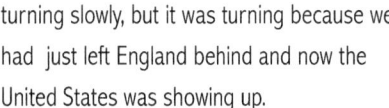

turning slowly, but it was turning because we had just left England behind and now the United States was showing up.

Now that, concluded The Pump Boy, was state-of-the-art publishing — or maybe more. In any case, or every case, it was a great feature to have the cool car and the hip publication in front of the shop. Good for business. Street traffic was slow these days. Walk-ins were rare. Heck, just seeing someone on the street around here was getting thin.

Rad looked at the building. There was a layer of suitably grey Gothic grime on every-thing. The glass windows facing the street may as well have been plates of pale slate. They had lost their transparency --not that there was anything to look at behind them. Even Rad didn't know.

The Pump Boy rubbed a little bit of window clean and peered inside: it was old-industri-ally boring. There were chairs and desks, and papers stacked about, an old lunch box, and a chart on the wall — a sort of graph with a jagged line on it that went up and down like a mountain range.

This one mainly went down, though.

Rad rubbed off some more grime, creating the words "OPEN" and "BELOW."

He drew some musical notes: a string of eighth notes — because that's what most people think music looks like. He then descended into the coruscating underworld of the musical instrument repair shop.

Rad entered the shop, and Largo spun around on her chair to greet him, a gleaming piccolo in hand. Her hair flew out a little from the centrifugal force. It was an unusual look — for her hair to move like that. Rad smiled, and Largo said something pretty but completely impossible to understand.

[70] TRPB 165.355.4163
Scraps of paper indicate that this
was part of a song written by
Campbell himself, while in high
school. Composed in C-minor.

[71] TRPB 165.355.4163
"I miss my homeland."

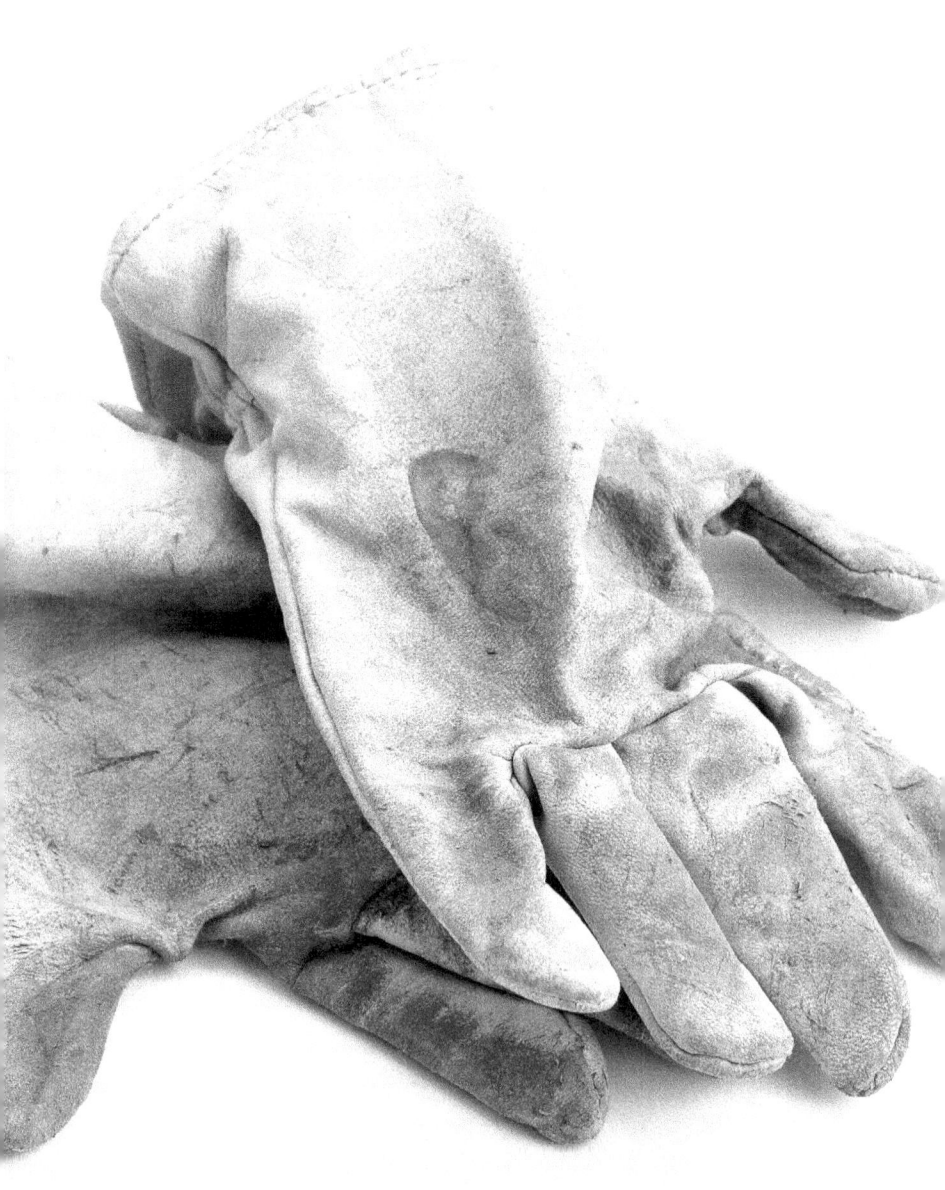

And that's when he noticed.

For the first time ever: Largo's hair was dry.

It still had that cool, Vanessa-Redgrave-from-the-movie-*Blow-Up* look, but it was dry this morning. And Rad had rather liked the wet hair look. Oh well.

This was good, too. If there was one thing that you could say about The New Girl, it was that she sure looked sophisticated, like a woman from the big city, but an even bigger city.

Rad wandered back to his workbench and flipped on the radio. Some guy was strumming an acoustic guitar and singing:

Swim in my foreign sea,
Stay right close to me.
There're so many things to see,
When you're ... with me.

"Boy, that's a strange way to put things," The Pump Boy murmured, reaching for a tuning wrench.

Fly in a whole new sky,
And never-ever have to cry
I'll tell you why:
Our world together ... doesn't lie. [70]

"Oh no. This guy needs a therapy session and a lesson on the suspended fourth. Listen to all those major chords — *la-la la-da-dee la-la-lah* — In a way, there is something scary about it," The Pump Boy proclaimed as he switched off the radio.

"Where's Bartók when you need him?"

Rad began putting the finishing touches on an old chromatic harp that he had recently re-strung. The chromatic harp doesn't have any pedals like a regular double-action harp, but it's still a big job to tune one.

As Rad was finishing the tuning job, he began to pluck a few notes, doing his best to recall the Bartók for which he had so recently pined. He was marveling at the novel melodic inferences in Bartók's "Scetches VII," when he caught a flash of light across the room.

There in the door was Largo Lips, with the mirror-polished piccolo. There was a damp streak down the side of her face, and from what it looked like, maybe more to come.

"Gee, I'm sorry," the Pump Boy said, "Did I disturb you? I was just fooling around with this thing."

"*Ma patrie... je la manque beaucoup,*" [71] she said.

Then as suddenly as she had appeared, she was off again. Gone.

"Zut" is a French colloquial expression meaning *damn all, shoot, crap*, et c.

"Man, Rad said. Maybe this not being able to understand each other isn't as cool as I thought. I didn't know it would cause normal people to start acting like space aliens."

Uh-oh. She was back for act two. But at least this time she had left the piccolo behind. Had it turned into a fight, that piccolo could have been dangerous – I mean, it's a small instrument, sure, but there isn't much you can do with a harp in retaliation.

Rad braced himself.

One time Fuzzy had batted at him for no reason whatsoever. Several times, come to think of it. It always seemed totally insane, but not a good kind of insane like the hurdy-gurdy guy with the make-believe monkey.

Largo Lips approached slowly and held her little glowing photograph of the beach in the mountains of the moon. She handed it to Rad.

"Well, that was close," The Pump Boy said as he took the little photo in his hands, "You sure had me worried."

It certainly was a nice photo.

From the very start, it had been an intensely odd sort of photo, glowing, as it did. But it was going from odd to weird. To even more weird. If you tilted it to the right, the picture would change, as if you were turning your head. Now that's cool. Seems there's a lot of new photo stuff

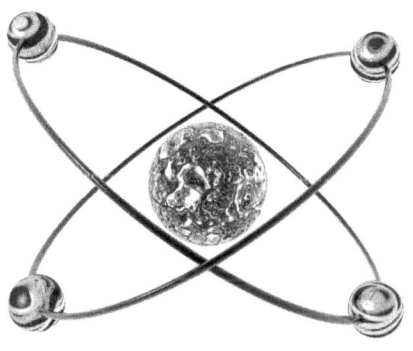

coming out these days.

And, let's see: if you tilted it to the left, your head turned the other way. Rad panned left. And way off to the side was a striking woman standing on a beach at the little bay. It was Largo Lips. She was smiling and wearing a bathing suit. Hmmmm ...

"Zut!!" she said, reaching quickly and tapping her own image.[72] The bathing suit instantly changed into a long sundress.

"Far out," Rad whispered.

The Pump Boy was tempted to touch the image again, and adjust it to his liking. But that didn't seem polite.

Behind the now fully dressed Largo was what looked like a blanket on the ground, and off to one side was a path, a stone cottage, some palm trees, sheep, lots of rocks. Rocks had obviously taken over this place. "Just like what's gonna happen here," Rad thought. "Just like what happened in Gob a' Gheodha." And there was also something very shiny beside the path.

"That's my homeland."

It was hard to see what it was since the sun was reflecting off the shiny thing — the way sun does sometimes.

"Thanks," Rad said, handing back the little photo. "That's cool. Except for the *zut* part."

"Zut ... ha!," she said, *"C'est ma patrie."*[73]

Largo turned and swooshed out of the workshop. It was nice: she was smiling again.

But how a little harp music and a high-tech photo could cause someone to cry was beyond the Pump mind.

These are beautiful, fascinating things: the world's oldest instrument and newest imaging technology. Now, that's gotta be a fun time, right?

Maybe women that you couldn't understand were just as mysterious as those you could — meaning the language.

Gosh, just when you start to figure things out, a new idea comes along and changes everything. No wonder the hurdy-gurdy man talks to an imaginary monkey. What if the monkey isn't imaginary after all? No wonder Hammering Jim pounds on his steering wheel and Karl carries his wipe-up rag like a baby's blanket. No wonder KillFlash doesn't even have a patrol car. No, it wasn't just

Rad. It was everyone who never knew the answers to the questions that bugged them the most.

Moe maybe being the exception. But only because questions didn't bug Moe.

Moe seemed to think that he could figure anything out if he thought about it long enough. This would never work for Rad. The more he thought about something, the less sense it made. Even simple questions became hallucinogenic diving platforms over the great unknown ...

Speaking of which, it was time to meet Moe at the shop. Moe was never on time himself, but he seemed to like it when Rad was punctual.

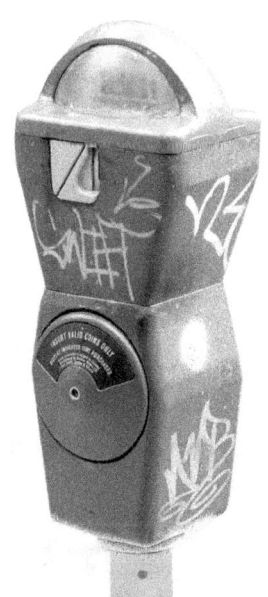

CHAPTER 30

**Helicopters drone
Slapping the sky
They won't go home**

**I wish I could fly
Fly away home**

**Helicopters drone
They never go home**

← ⟶ ○

Rad looked around in the garage and saw a telltale smoke signal rising from a small skateboard car at the back of the shop.

"Moe, what's up?"

"Oh, pulling the exhaust off this 964. Can't change the plugs otherwise."

"Wow," Rad said as he approached the half of Moe that wasn't under the car, "What are ya doing down there?"

"That's where the plugs are in this car, Rad, at least half of them anyway."

"And the other half?"

"Well, you have to get them from the top. And that's not easy either."

"Sounds like a lot of work, Moe. Complicated, huh?"

ATR Moe slid out from under the car, sat up, and took his cigar out of his mouth — this usually means more than a short answer.

"Rad, you drive a Rambler. It is a very simple machine. These machines are complex, complicated, and very tightly packaged. The result is a level of performance that can be realised only by someone either very skilled or very foolhardy."

The Pump Boy scratched his head: "What's the point, Moe?"

"I don't know how to put it, Rad. This car is like a fine pipe organ. Your car is like a harmonica."

"I get it," Rad said, "You can't put a pipe organ in your back pocket and take it to the beach."

Moe stood up and walked over to his workbench. The hafnium was still there,

74 TRPB 535.115.4000
In the manner of the composer Brian Eno,
known for his ethereal works.

75 TRPB 535.115.4000
While left-foot braking is usually the sign of
an inept driver, the technique is used in racing
the older Porsche turbos. The idea is to keep
the throttle open to maintain boost pressure.

and the little chrome music player.

"I want you to listen to something," Moe said, picking up the chrome box and untangling the miniature headphones.

Moe pressed the solitary button on the box and handed the headphones to Rad.

Rad could hear the Enoesque[74] melody even before he had the headphones on.

He listened. It was the same recording that he had heard before: a haunting development in fugue on what sounded like an antique pipe organ. There was a lot of echo, as if recorded in a cathedral.

"What is it?" Moe asked.

"I don't know."

"Come on, Rad, it's a pipe organ like that pile of junk that you have, isn't it?"

Rad took the headphones off, but didn't push the button. "Oh, yeah, of course. It's a big organ, old. I thought that you meant the composition. I thought that I knew every organ piece on the planet."

"Maybe you do."

****

"That's what I wanted to talk to you about, Rad," Moe said, putting the cigar back in its usual place and disappearing into a smoke world, "What did ya wanna talk to me about?"

"Well, uh, check me if I'm wrong, Moe. But I think we weren't quite finished with that last discussion?"

"We'll come back to it."

It sounded like Moe had a plan, driving the conversation as if he were driving a car. Shifting gears, downshifting, left-foot braking: Moe stuff.[75] May as well go along with the plan.

After all, Rad didn't have one. Or, he wasn't aware of one.

"Moe, I turned the water off. There's a spaceship. And it was always being rained on by a hydrant, you know. But I turned it off. I think you can fix it. I guess it's probably more complicated than a 964, but I was thinking of the old days. You know ... the phone booth thing."

Rad was out of things to say.

Silence.

Maybe Moe didn't have a plan after all.

"It's more than the mechanical complications, Rad. I know about the spacecraft."

"You do?"

"It belongs to a customer," Moe said, putting his finger on the sliver of hafnium, "Where do you think this came from?"

"Space?"

[76] TRPB 165.355.4163
Tate conjecture, similar to Hodge conjecture, is an unsolved math problem involving shaping of equations.

[77] TRPB 165.355.4163
Your turn, gifted reader. Of course it means something.

"The owner of that spacecraft wants me to fix it for her. I've already looked at it."

"When it was raining?"

"Yeah, she came in one day — to Larry's. Of course, it's impossible to understand these aliens."

"Well, what about those napkin-eating chain smokers that you hang out with?" Rad asked.

"I'm picking up a little of the language. But we usually communicate with drawings and formulae. A quadratic equation is a quadratic equation, after all. These guys are good. The one showed me the solution to the Tate conjecture.[76] No kidding. So I know a few words. Anyway, this lady comes in all soaking wet. Seemed a bit odd."

Rad heard the click of a light bulb switch.

"Wet hair?"

"Of course."

"Pretty?"

"Um ... well ... yes. Very, in fact," Moe said, "Rad, come on, she works for you."

"The New Girl? But she drives an old Citroën, not a spaceship. A girl, driving a spaceship? I ... I don't understand, Moe."

"Well, it's not always possible to understand things instantly. Even with a rabbit trap mind like yours."

The light bulb was still on, but it was obviously going to take some time.

Besides, skateboard cars were lining up outside: thirsty. Moe's was the only station in town that had high-octane gas — when he had gas — and the skateboard cars never drank anything else.

"Moe, I'm gonna go pump some gas. I need to let this soak in over some fumes."

"Rad," Moe said, "We still have to go back to that unfinished conversation."

"Oh, about the organ music?"

"Yes."

"Not now, Moe. I have to ... uh ... get used to what I now understand. Right?"

"Good idea. You pump some gas. I change some plugs. We run down to Larry's for a break."

"Thanks, Moe. But ... uh, one other question. What's Largo Lips' real name?."

"Sorry, Rad. She doesn't have one. Aliens just have a number: they're socialists."

"Well, what's her number?"

"It doesn't matter."

"It matters to me."

"Uh ... 7734-514."[77]

"Thank you."

[78] TRPB 165.355.4163
In this Rad graffito, which may be in quotations because he is using phrases that he hears from the drivers, the items listed are actually technical phrases that describe components of a high-performance engine. The "waste gates" pop open when a turbo-charged engine is at full boost; combine this with hot (street-compatible) camshaft grind, and indeed, you would leave the rest of the world behind. The pressure-fed "tensioners" keep the cam chain from jumping.

[79] TRPB 165.355.4163
Rad is referring to the giant man-eating (and probably radioactive) blob from the 1958 sci-fi movie of the same name. There was a remake in 1988, but Rad is thinking of the 1958 film because "Nothing can stop it!" is a tagline from the movie's promo.

CHAPTER 31

"Pressure-fed tension
And Street-compatible grind.
Waste gates pop off,
Leaving the world behind." [78]

Rad tried to make sense of the skateboard talk. The car-brain people were pleasant and excited about everything in general. Especially their rather musical cars — even though the music was more like tribal drumming than roving strings. Though, excitable and pleasant as they were, they seldom made much sense: isn't all tension pressure fed? And what's behind a waste gate? Not a pleasant thought. Mildly disturbing, in fact.

Rad kept looking around as he filled the tanks, concerned that the waste gates would pop open and some protoplasmic thing like The Blob would appear, oozing toward them. Nothing can stop it! [79] It would show up as a glow and reveal itself between two buildings, consuming everything in its insatiable and slimy, self-absorbed advance upon life as we know it. Krikey! And of course, like everything else around here lately, it would be from outer space.

No wonder these skateboards wanted to leave the world behind.

Sometimes the idea had its merits.

The cars made a lot of heat.

Standing in the heat, thinking about The Blob, inhaling high-octane fumes, hair gel starting to melt. It was easy to work up a thirst under such conditions.

Rad picked up the yellow and red "NO GAS. SORRY" sign, hung it on the pumps, and went into the garage.

[80] TRPB 165.355.4163
Little Nemo in Slumberland was
a phantasmagorical comic strip
drawn by Windsor McKay in the
early 20th century. Victor
Moscoso, later in the 20th
century, drew complex
psychedelic comic strips,
some of which included
Little Nemo (Zap #6). McKay,
by the way, not Disney, is the
father of the animated cartoon.

"Hey Moe! You done?"

An answer in the affirmative came from somewhere.

"Hey Moe, what's behind a waste gate?" "Pressurized by-products of combustion, nitrogen and carbon dioxide and monoxide. The same stuff that comes out of a normal exhaust."

"Like a car exhaust?"

"Yes, Rad," Moe said as he appeared out of the dark. "Why? Did all that exhaust gas make you thirsty?"

"I guess you could say that."

"Well, let's go."

Larry's Limited Slip was dark and noisy. The pump eyes were still adjusting to the dark, but the pump ears already heard the bizarre sound of the alien language.

"You get a couple of drafts from Larry, and I'll be right back," Moe said.

Larry was wearing his traditional toque with the outdated lettering. "So, Rad, did the Skyrockets to the Blue Moons put you in orbit?"

"Orbit was good, Larry," replied the RPB, "thanks. But I forgot about re-entry. That's probably the worst part of a space ride, isn't it?"

"Well, it's only once in a blue moon for you," Larry said, evidently having found something amusing.

"They would make men believe that the moon is made of green cheese," The Pump Boy said, "Isn't that the old saying? But there is no green cheese, so I think they meant blue cheese."

"What are you trying to say, Rad? That the moon is made of blue cheese?"

"I don't know, Larry, I've never been there."

"You ever seen those old cartoons where the moon has a face on it and can talk?"

"Sure. I love that stuff ... Little Nemo meets Victor Moscoso." [80]

"Huh? Neither of'em comes in here, Rad. Well, that's a blue moon. Only a blue moon can do that."

"Well, Larry. It's just gonna be two ice-cold ones today. Moe and I are on a break from a busy day at the garage."

"Looks like Moe's talking with the neutrino necktie set again."

"Oh, he'll be back, Larry, I know his type."

Larry placed the two mugs in front of The Pump Boy and moved away to the left, wiping the bar as he cruised.

Moe came over to the bar with a napkin covered with equations, doodles, and alien words. Some of the doodles were pretty good. There was something wrapped inside the napkin.

[81] TRPB 651.914.9244
A beignet is a French form of doughnut (sold in the U.S. by that name in New Orleans).

"Rad, I need you to really focus for this one," Moe said.

The Pump Boy downed the top half of his beer and said, "I am really focused."

"Do you know what this is?," Moe said, pushing the doodle-covered napkin an inch or two in Rad's direction.

Rad looked.

"Moe ... I'm on board with this. It's ... it's a napkin."

Moe lightly slapped the back of the porcupine-quill head: "Not the napkin! Open it!"

Rad carefully unwrapped the napkin and stared at the contents. For the first time, Rad wondered whether Moe, beat poet, master mechanic, and an organ head into unknown music, had finally lost his mind --which is easy enough to do.

"Moe," he said, "Okay. I see what you mean. This is a little different. But I know what it is. Yep. This looks like a doughnut that had a few too many Blue Moons and fell down in a patch of confectioner's sugar on the way home. This is a drunk doughnut wrapped in a napkin, a napkin covered with alien doodles. Ya see, I know that I sometimes I view things differently from other people, but I'm pretty sure I'm on target with this."

"Really?"

"Yep. Though I would never use that word myself."

"Well, that's a good thing, Rad. Because you are off the mark on this one. Not on target, not on the paper. Not even on the range. Listen up: this is not a doughnut."

(Rad waited)

(Moe waited)

Moe finally rapped the drunken doughnut with two fingers and said, "This ... is a beignet!"

(Rad waited again)

"How do you spell that, Moe?"
"B-E-I-G-N-E-T"
"That spells ben-YAY?"
"Not in our language. It's an alien word, Rad. It's the alien word for fuel. This beignet, here," Moe said, rapping again, "is the alien equivalent to high-octane gas." [81]

Moe leaned back, arms akimbo.
It was nice to see Moe so content.
But the victory and mission architecture were vague — at least so far.

"Is this thing important to us, Moe?"
"Only to you, Rad, only to you. And if I were you, it would be important to me."

TRPB 535.115.4000
Moe has picked up some alien slang,
not school French, meaning "don't talk
nonsense" or "give me a break!"

CHAPTER 32

Two more beers please.
One for me,
One for Moe:
And then we'll go.

"Moe, I thought we were gonna talk about organ music. Not bakery products."

"This is not a bakery product, Rad. It just looks like one. Just one of these numbers here and you have escape velocity: 25 thousand miles per hour. Besides. I don't know any more about organ music than you know about spider gears."

"Isn't that escape speed? But ... but the organ music? You listen to it?"

"Those guys gave me that recording," Moe said, jerking his head toward the smoky corner full of bad-tie foreign-planet types.

"Problem is: the last old organ burned up on their plant. They're shoppin' for one here. But so far, no deals."

"Well, that's too bad. It took me a long time to find mine."

Rad noticed that the chain-smoking paper-chewers were watching the conversation. He couldn't help thinking of the praying mantis.

"Moe, you didn't tell these guys that I had a nineteenth-century pipe organ, did you? Like the one on that recording?"

Moe's head turned in the direction of his boots. Not good.

"Moe! What if these guys have ray guns, robots, man-absorbing mirrors — maybe even a Blob?"

"Faut pas déconner, non?![82] They gave up weapons centuries ago. And they can't get a bank loan because they gave up

83 TRPB 165.355.4163
Another phrase taken from
street lingo, meaning, basically,
"pad the bill."

finance too."

"Because of being socialists?"

"I don't know. But no one would give them a loan here. I mean ... they are aliens, after all."

"That's discrimination. Let's call Hammering Jim!"

"No. Can't. Lawyers are forbidden in their society."

"Oh? But antique organs are worth the danger of re-entry?"

"Evidently."

Rad picked up his beer and took some thoughtful gulps.

"Well, Moe, these guys sound okay, I guess. I'd like to help. But if they don't have finance and loans and stuff, what do they have?"

Moe glanced over his shoulder: a number of the aliens were nodding their heads at him, leaning forward. Poor guys. They looked so hopeful. Look at how excited they were!

"Rad," Moe said, finally looking up from the trusty boots, "they use a barter system."

"Barter system? So, uh, they're from outer space. They must have some cool stuff."

"Oh, nothing that we can use. That's the problem. Just some advanced imaging technology and plenty of alien fuel."

"Alien fuel? You mean those benyays?"

"Yeah."

"Yah see," Moe said," they brought a cargo ship here, figuring they'd need it to haul the pipe organ. The thing is loaded with fuel. Rows and rows of the little buggers! It's a big ship. You've probably seen it. It's disguised as an old diner on the corner of the sector. Brightly polished stainless steel, but kinda dirty right now."

"Oh yeah. Real art deco thing? With the music name ... um ... "Note all Sale," or something?"

Moe leaned forward.

"That's the one! But it's ... um ... *"Sale la Note"* – doesn't have anything to do with music. [83] It's a joke about finance, I think. But anyway, well, that's where I got the idea for the neon apron under the gas islands."

"Cool, Moe. Yeah, come to think of it. That thing has a glow underneath it too."

"Yeah, but it isn't neon."

There was a pause and some beer sipping.

"Rad, please allow me to illuminate something."

"That's a good idea, Moe, I'm starting to lose track of all the pieces."

"That alien fuel has no value to anyone on this planet ... except you."

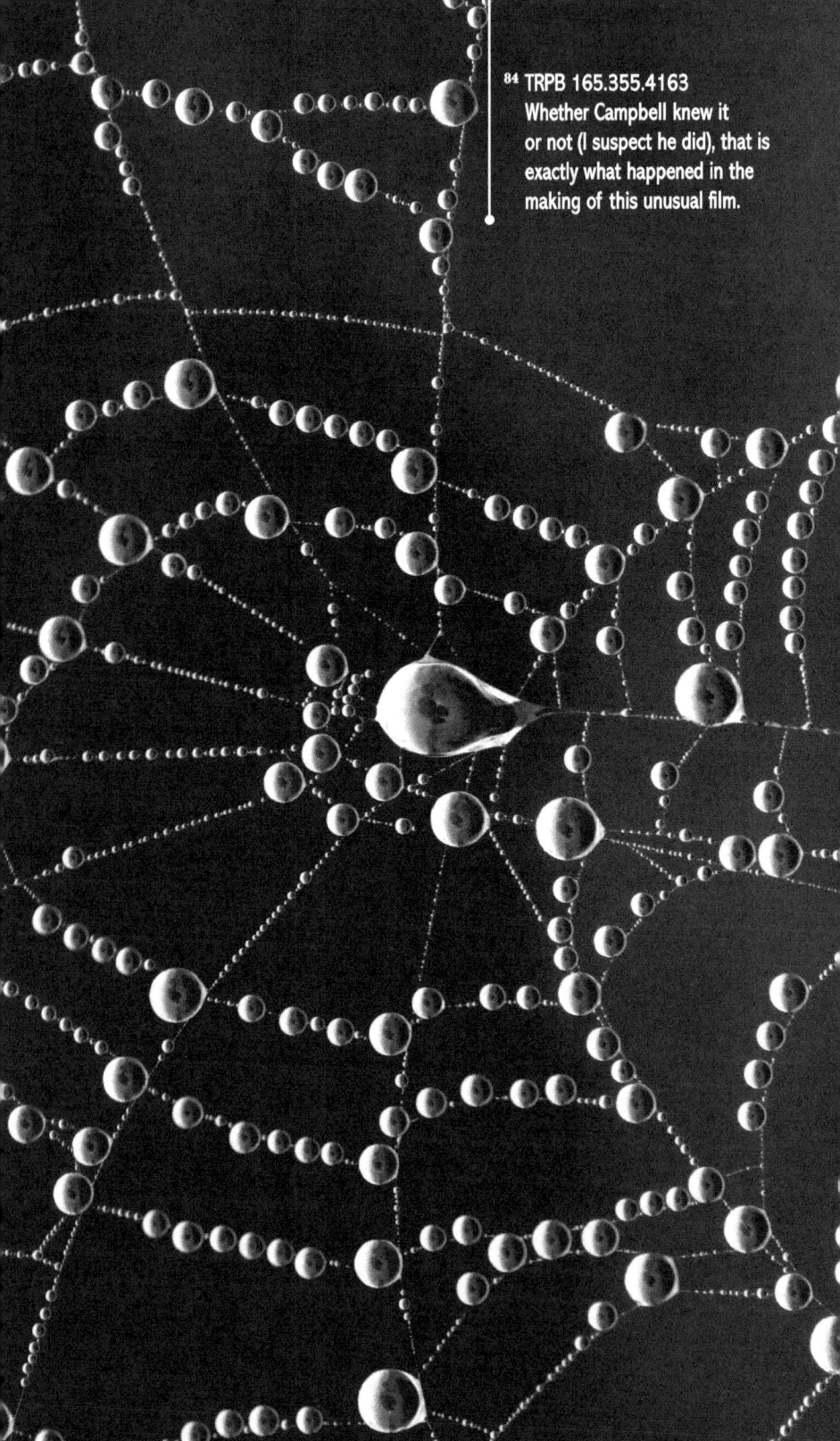

84 TRPB 165.355.4163
Whether Campbell knew it
or not (I suspect he did), that is
exactly what happened in the
making of this unusual film.

The Pump Head was 1. not in its best form today, 2. rather drained from the heat, and 3. in possession of entirely too much new information. It was gonna take some time to figure out where all this was going.

If only he had seen the movie.

"Moe?"

"Yeah."

"What happened at the end of the movie, *Man from Planet X*? Do you know?"

"Of course I know, but I think that they ran out of shooting time and had to rush the plot.[84] It's not a reliable indicator."

"Did the man from Planet X have weapons?"

"No. He was doing okay until the bad guys got on his nerves, or tried to work him over, and then he used mind control — that was his only weapon. Um ... don't get excited about this, but I think that he turned a lot of people into killer zombies. But this is a different movie, Rad. That stuff was all make believe."

"Well, I hadn't even thought about killer zombies. That would be bad. Okay. Fair enough, I guess, Do you think Largo Lips — or whatever her number is — has mind control?"

"Rad, I don't mean to sound like Hemingway on ya, but there can be the appearance of mind control coming from another when it is just your own mind being a dope. So, maybe yes, maybe no. The moral question is intentionality."

Just then, Larry came around interjecting, "Hemingway never said anything like that. What he did say was that the check shall always be presented. One of the swell things you can count on."

And with that, Larry left a slip of paper on the bar, and the two intergalactic barter officers started digging into their pockets.

WATCHING
THE ASHES OF
GOMORRAH

CHAPTER 33

Exciting smells
Unless you're weary.
In the garage
It's dark and dreary.

"Should I man the pumps, Moe?"

"Nah, we're out of gas."

Oops — an ethical dilemma. Rad wasn't sure whether or not to mention that the "No Gas" sign had just been a bit of a convenience at the time.

Rad looked around the garage. It was an orderly garage with everything in its place. It was Moe's world. There were a lot of tools and books, and what looked like some science experiments, too.

"Moe, on the subject of gas ... "

"Ha! You beat me to it, Rad."

"Oh, well, by all means, please ... um ... elucidate further."

"Look, Rad. I can work a deal with my pals there in the bar for your pipe organ. It's an unproductive asset for you. Jim says you're upside down on it."

"I kinda picked up on that, Moe, but the organ is a good thing. It's a happy thing."

"Rad, it's a non-thing."

The Pump Boy sat down on a nearby car lift. How could anything be a non-thing? How could something good be a non-thing? Moe talked ... um ... so specifically sometimes, and about so many concepts at once, that it was often hard to follow him. Not that he didn't know what he was talking about, no. But sometimes Rad felt that listening was like reaching for a glass that had already fallen from the table.

However, Moe was a natural leader: because he was always going somewhere.

OK. Enough for now.

"Where are we going with this, Moe?"

"Rad, remember how we were talking about Hemingway?"

"I wasn't really following that very well, Moe. I'm sorry. It seemed kind of sad. I want to know why the organ is a non-thing?"

"But it's all connected, Rad. You even said so yourself once."

"... Um ... I need some lines between the dots, Moe. I'm good at tic-tac-toe — I always win — but connect the dots is tough, especially because I reject number theory."

"Rad, the organ is a musical instrument, but what you have is a stack of crates."

"You sound like Jim."

"Same words perhaps, but with an entirely different plan."

"Jim's plan Is to sell the organ."

"That's my plan, too."

"More lines, Moe. I'm starting to see double."

"Jim just wants more cash on the balance sheet. With my plan, you don't have to worry about the balance sheet. There won't be one."

Rad tried once more to imagine the use of a balance sheet, which to him was something like a magic carpet: just floating in the air, poised perfectly on something invisible.

"Look at me, Rad. You told me once why you didn't want to sell the organ, remember?"

"Yeah."

"Tell me again. Tell me why."

The Pump Head knew that this was important. People often tried to get you to answer questions and derive conclusions — it was one of the more nightmarish and torturous of school memories. These exercises seemed to be constructed to shelter you from the truth — as if anyone really knew in the first place.

Moe lit a cigar and sat down directly across from the RPB, smoking ... and waiting.

"I have all day," Moe said.

"Was what I said right, Moe, about the organ?"

"Right. Wrong. Sing a song. I don't know. It was suitable. That's why I'm gonna sit here until I hear it again."

The smoky cloud made thinking easier and more relaxing. It was a pleasant place to be: no cars outside, no customers, no Blob or killer zombies — at least, not yet.

[85] TRPB 535.115.4000
Contorted paraphrasing from Hemingway.

[86] TRPB 535.115.4000
Soixante-dix-sept trente quatre:
French for 7734.

Time passed.

(Half a cigar later)

"Moe, what I said about the organ was that I read somewhere once ... that when you had an emptiness, and that emptiness was caused by something bad, that it would fill up on its own. But when it was caused by losing something good, it could only be filled up again by something better."

"Do you believe that?," Moe asked. "Do you remember where you read that?"[85]

Rad was nervous about all this thinking. Thinking usually led to trouble. And trouble usually led to Larry's Limited Slip.

"I guess I believe it enough to not trade my organ for money."

"Trade?" Moe questioned, "Interesting word."

The Pump Boy knew that ATR Moe was steering again and shifting gears. Why?

"Rad, let me ask you something."
"Sure, Moe."

"Would something better possibly be a free ride through outer space to an alien beach? With 7734-514?"

"One more line, please, Moe."

"Rad, I checked over the spacecraft: there's nothing wrong with it. A few minor dings and some hafnium repair. But the deal is that — and go easy on this — looks like 7734-514 just ran out of gas."

"Gas? Largo Lips? ..."

"Alien fuel, Rad."

"Benyays?"

Moe removed his cigar: "Yes, beignets."

Rad drew an image in the air, connecting all the dots.

"Moe, is this why you said that if you were me that it would be important to you?"

Moe extinguished his barely potent cigar and wandered off to a toolbox: "Yeah, Rad, that's why I said that. I'm gonna deal with these guys tonight. I'll get as a much fuel as you are going to need — for 7734."

"That's her nickname?"

"Kind of. The second number is just a modifier, even though it comes after the first number. They go backwards, ya know."

"Should I call her 7734?"

"No, Rad ... It doesn't sound like that in her language. It sounds completely different, just like everything else."

"What does it sound like, Moe?"

Moe started to roll his eyes, but checked them," Best that I can figure, something like *Swasant dees eht trahnt khat rah.*"[86]

TRPB 165.355.4163
Ginsberg was a leader of the
Beat Movement (1950s),
which included Kerouac,
Cassady, and Burroughs.
Ginsberg, later in life, really
did lead entire auditoriums full
of people into singing mantras.

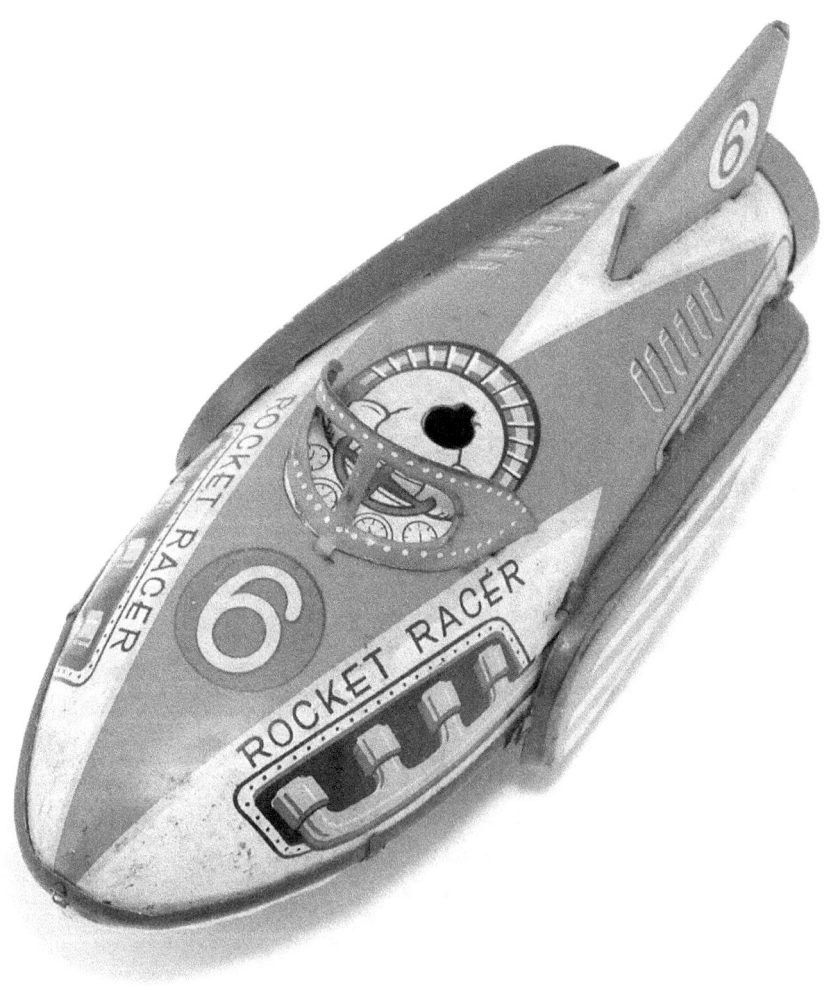

"Oh, I see. Sort of. Is that like Hindu? It sure sounds like the start of a nifty mantra. Check it out:

Swasant dees eht ...
swasant dees eht trahnt ...
swasant dees eht trahnt khat rah ...
... trahnt khat rah."

[silence]

"Rad, listen. I mean, that's a good mantra. It really is, and you have the timing down perfectly. Heck, you could be Allen Ginsberg, [87] really. But we have other things to focus on. These guys are going to be at Larry's tonight, and they are going to have the fuel, the beignets. I need some paperwork from Hammering Jim."

"Do I have to go to his office?"

"Well, yes. Soon. "

"Ok, Moe. I don't like that place, but I'll go. So, may I come to Larry's tonight?"

This time, Moe rolled his eyes for real.

"That's what Largo Lips — uh, *Swasant dees eht trahnt khat rah* — says all the time, too, Moe. What's up there. What are you guys looking at?"

"Beats me," Moe said. "Do you believe that the universe is infinite?"

"I'm not sure. I think that it's spherical in nature and doesn't relate to number theory."

"So does it have a dimension?"

"Of course not, Moe."

"Well then, there must be a lot of stuff up there — like everything."

"Up there. Down there. It's all the same at the pogo fair," The Rad head was starting to bob up and down.

Moe watched acidulously while poking around in his toolbox and finally closing the lid with a pronounced, metallic *whap!*

"Rad, you said that you're on board with this. I'm gonna get the beignets tonight. I'm going to bring them to you at the bar at Larry's. They don't improve with age, so get them to 7734 first thing in the morning."

"She'll know what to do?'

"She'll know what to do."

"You don't want me in on the deal?"

"Rad, you just hang with Larry. Larry's okay. Really he is."

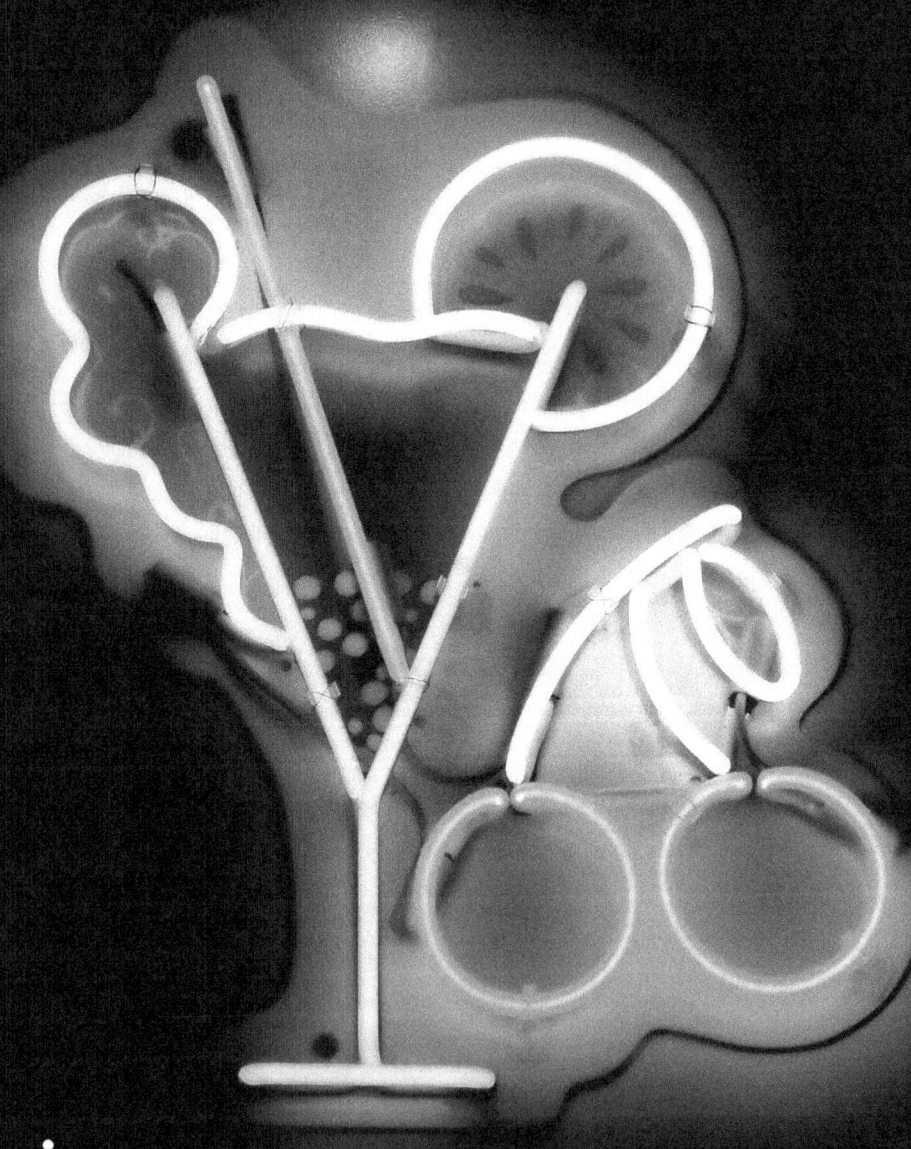

88 TRPB 535.115.4000
A real cocktail, raspberry liqueur and
Blue Curacao with Champagne to make
it take off. WARNING: do not drink these!

CHAPTER 34

Out of the clutch of the rabbit hutch,
Let's see what's here: nibble far and nibble near,
jump and play
ever farther away.
And with a little luck, we'll learn to duck.
Run rabbit run:
Or never see the sun.

Too much thinking and planning. And long after the sun had set, it was time for a visit to Larry's Limited Slip.

Just as Rad had suspected.

Moe and the chain-smoking foreign planet types — now confirmed aliens — were drinking hard and slapping each other on the back and saying things that no one could understand.

Rad stuck to the plan, though.

Even though the plan was changing by the minute, eventually leading to Rad's creating his own drink called the Cosmic Adventure. Larry claimed that it was pretty much the same thing as a Volcano, [88] but Rad wasn't so sure. He thought that it was the perfect combination of colour and bubbles.

Art and adventure.
Have head, will travel.
Let reality unravel.

Larry interrupted, "Hey Rad, it's getting late. Maybe the Cosmic Adventure has come to a close."

"Hardly, Larry."

Funny as it sounds, Rad had forgotten that he was in a public place. His world had been shrinking. The sphere constricting. He couldn't get the image of a thimble out of his head — and there was so much other stuff in there to begin with. A world so small, you could have dropped it in a thimble. And never see it again.

"Rad? You still with the program here?"

It was Moe. He looked tired and even ... well, maybe even a bit distrustful.

"Rad, are you good to get home?

"I'm fine, Moe. Larry and I were just going ..."

"Here," Moe said, sliding a waxed white paper bag under Rad's forearm. "Take this to the shop tomorrow."

165

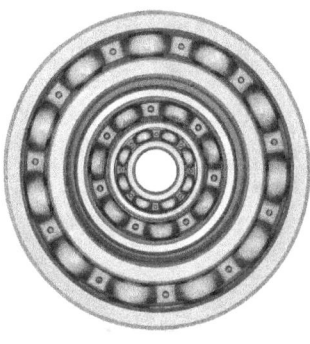

CHAPTER 35

**When you're up all night
and the windows glow,
You're afraid to look out
because ...
... you know.**

Rad awoke to the metallic groans of a garbage truck wrestling with its dumpster associate somewhere farther down the street. There may have been two or three of them, or it may have just been so many echoes. The sounds were mournful, almost combative, as if struggling toward finality — like the last movement of an iron symphony.

The Pump Boy tumbled out of bed and peeked outside. It was already busy out there. There were the garbage trucks, cars passing, a few people on foot, men with air hammers and hard hats, a grey sky, and low clouds picking their way through the tops of the taller buildings. He could even see one of the garbage trucks, which was creaking and banging and even rocking a bit. Several men in uniform were pushing and shoving at the dumpster that the truck was attempting to engage. Maybe the dumpster didn't want to go?

But you could tell that it would have to go.

That's what the men in uniform did: they made you go.

rhymes with pick-up sticks
closer to home
let's cast the bones

The alien fuel was safe on the night-stand: ready for delivery and ready for an adventure well beyond the curvature of the Earth, the mountains of the moon, the planets of the sun, and the planets of the stars unseen.

"That's quite a trip."

Rad looked on the floor for something interesting to wear, but soon settled on his Known Water Authority uniform. It was a one-piece design, so it was pretty easy to pull together: just climb in and fasten. There was a hat that went with it as well, two hats: one for wearing above ground, and one for wearing below ground, even though practically no one went underground (reflecting on his adventures underground, Rad could understand). Neither hat happened to be in sight, however, and there was hardly any time to look for them.

The usual layer of dusty grime covered the Rambler's windshield —and, everything else. As it so often happens, someone had written a note in the grime.

"Travel ... Where ...?," questioned the note.

Rad was unsure whether to answer the question or just go ahead and clean the windshield. Did somebody really want to know? Was it just rhetorical? Or was it even meant to be clever?

"None of the above," Rad concluded, wiping the message into the oblivion of unanswered questions. "Some people want to know everything."

The Rambler sputtered to life and trembled mildly before settling down to its near-silent, belt-hiss idle.

Rad checked the positioning of the waxed white bag, moving it from the seat to the floor to reduce the chance of someone seeing it.

This was an important trip. It was up to Rad and the official Cosmic Ranger transport device to get the alien fuel to the shop without incident.

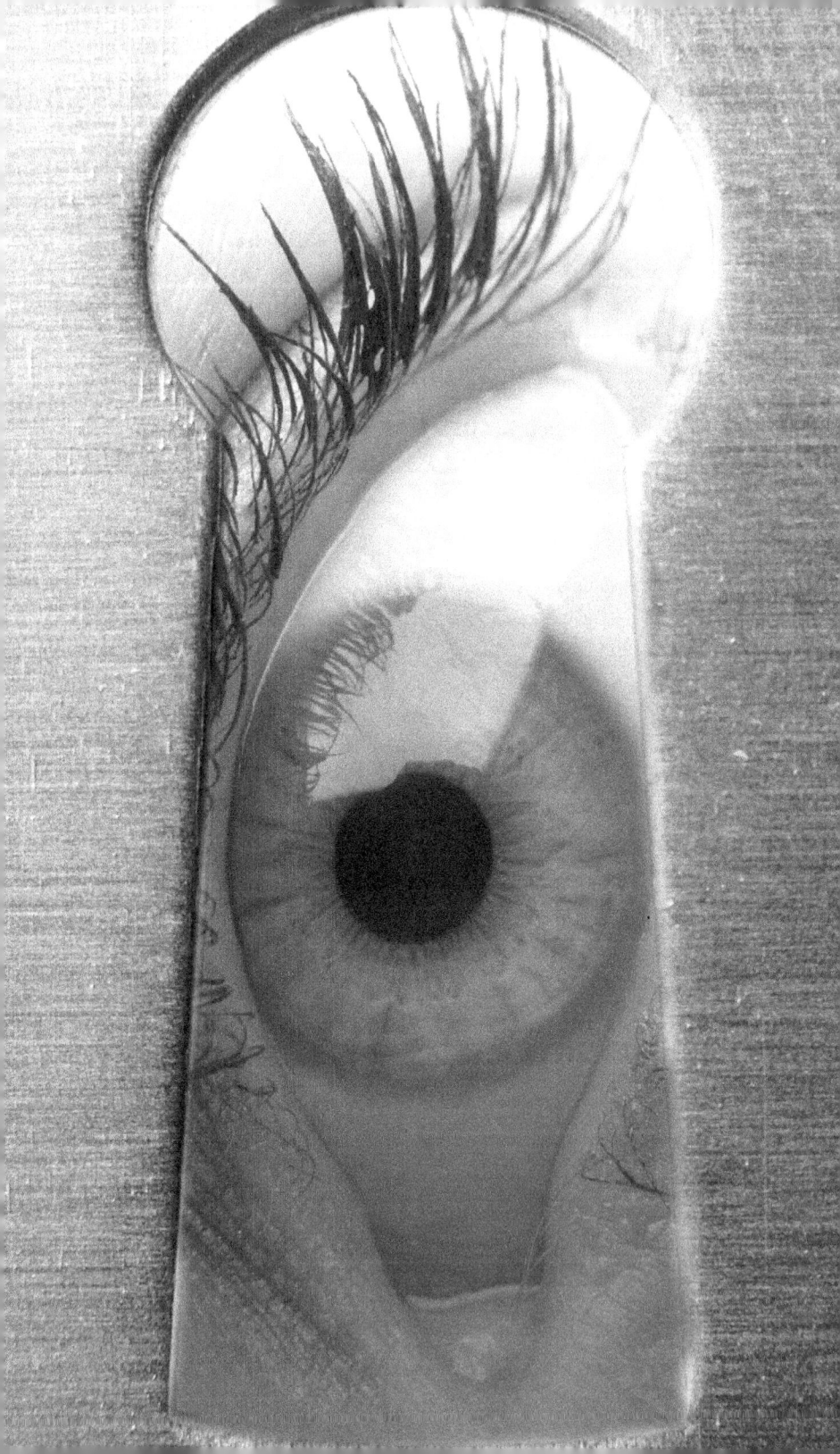

under the long hair of the moon
I never heard a nightingale
under the burning sun of noon
just crunch of long-dead snail

There was a parking spot directly in front of the shop. A large bit of architectural ornament — a chunk of marble frieze or cornice block or something — had fallen from above into the street. It looked very heavy and was somewhat buried in the pavement. Maybe people thought more parts would fall off.

"Inevitable," Rad said as he shrugged and backed the Rambler into a spot behind the fallen ornament. He grabbed the bag of fuel and entered the shop, noting that someone had added to the notes he had drawn on the shop window, literally. They had added some more eighth notes to Rad's string.

Inside, 7734 was pacing behind the counter, wringing her hands and speaking quietly to herself. When she saw Rad, she began waving her hands about and speaking rapidly in a wholly incomprehensible gibberish that was both frightening and melodic.

Rad shrugged. He smiled at her.

7734 shrugged too. She approached The Pump Boy slowly and took him by the hand, leading him into the back of the shop, stopping on the now empty floor where the oaken crates had once been piled. She looked at Rad and then started making odd sounds again, this time with even more gesticulation, pointing up, shrugging, shaking her head, and rocking her hips a bit.

"It's OK," Rad said, holding his finger to his lips, "Shhhh. It's OK. I know. I know all about it.

This succeeded in quieting things down a bit, and most of the motion came to a halt, with the exception of a slow back-and-forth movement of the head and a subdued rock of the hips.

"Now," Rad said, carefully taking her hand, which was still trembling ever so slightly, "There is something that I want to show you."

89 TRPB 165.355.4163
"I am saved."

90 TRPB 165.355.4163
"You're nuts! What an
absurd venture."

Rad led 7734 back to the front of the shop where she usually polished instruments. There was a French horn on the workbench, beautifully polished in all but one spot.

"Gosh, you do nice work," he said, "I wonder what you do back home. Other than stand around the beach half-naked?"

Rad looked at the little photograph. It had been adjusted back to its original view – at least, the one that Rad had first seen. He pointed to the photograph, and then placed the waxed white paper bag next to the French horn. He opened the bag and then motioned to it with his palm.

7734 approached the bag cautiously with her head up, following her nose, which was sniffing with increasing intensity as she hovered over the beignets. She peered inside. Her jaw dropped, leaving her mouth open.

"How exciting," Rad murmured.

"Je suis sauvé," [89] she said.

For a moment, she simply stood there: mouth open slightly, hair hanging down around her face, head still moving back and forth. Then she turned to Rad.

Rad pointed again at the picture and then pointed back himself, nodding his head. She pointed up at the ceiling, wrinkling her nose in a questioning manner.

Rad nodded, "There it goes, beyond the wires, into the trees. Where will it land? Nobody knows," doing his best pantomime of a flying spacecraft. Even though it probably didn't make sense to stick his arms out and wiggle them like wings since spaceships didn't have any.

"Tu es fou." She said, *"Quelle enterprise absurd."* [90]

"Zut!" Rad said, shrugging his shoulders and employing the only alien expression that he knew. Yet, recognizing a similar sounding and engaging word, he decided to add, *"Absurd. Yes. Zut! Absurd!"*

7734 laughed quietly as she removed the little photograph from the wall, picked up the bag of beignets, and tugged at The Pump Boy's sleeve.

As they were leaving the shop, Rad considered locking the door, but since

⁹¹ TRPB 165.355.4163
This is a pretty good description
of how mirror neurons work in the
human brain. The neurons reflect
the actions of others and are
responsible for empathy. This is
why seeing someone yawn makes
us yawn. They probably explain why
advertising works. In fact, mirror
neurons do allow people to
communicate even when they
do not share a common language,
but have a common culture or
value system.

⁹² TRPB 165.355.4163
"Follow me."

WOOHOO!

no one came in anyway and Jim had the Power of Attorney, certainly he could see through walls and open locked doors.

"I like the way your ship is decorated," he said, "all those mirrors on the inside. It looks like Karl's, or the inside of an alien's brain."

He looked. But she didn't appear to be offended, and was even walking briskly as if in a suppressed skip. Rad tried a little suppressed skip himself. It was kind of fun — as if dancing together without really admitting to it.

But 7734 didn't respond with any more than a smile, which was just fine.

"Maybe that's what the inside of my brain looks like too," the Pump Boy said. "How else would I know how much alike we are? Twin mirror collections talking to each other even when we can't." [91]

After a few blocks of ever less suppressed skipping and smiling, accompanied by the crackling rustle of the waxed paper bag, they turned the corner and saw the spacecraft, which was brighter and more reflective than ever before, looking itself like a giant cast curved mirror. It was magnificent.

"Must have been Moe," Rad said, stopping to admire his funhouse reflection. "Moe must have polished it. What a guy!"

"Suivez moi," [92] she said, tugging at the stationary Pump Boy.

She walked right into her own reflection in the side of the spacecraft. There was no door. Rad followed. They emerged from the mirror inside the spacecraft, just as Rad had supposed.

Boy, you sure know a lot more than you think you do, even when you're just guessing.

CHAPTER 38

**Have head will travel
Let the world unravel
It's fun to never know**

**Off we go
To the puppet show**

There was no rear-view mirror in the spacecraft, but there were portholes all around.

As The Pump Boy looked back over the curve of the Earth and the shadow of the moon, he saw a phone booth trailing behind them.

Real soon.

THE END
(for now)

VISUAL TRANSLATION

Artists whose images assisted in the visual translation of SunBurn:

Cover:	Radical Pump Boy	Andrej Godjevac
Page 2	Visual translation	Kirsty Pargeter
Page 3	Going forward	maggie
Page 6	Drumlegsticks	Alfredo Schaufelberger
Page 8	Smoking Fingernails	stockphoto
Page 11	Graphic hand	Bocos Benedict
Page 12	Rear View	Egidijus Mika
Page 13	Floating Heads	Jurgen Ziewe
Page 15	Ransom Type	Gina Goforth
Page 16	Drip, Drip, Drip	Milos Luzanin
Page 17	Communication	Alex Staroseltsev
Page 18	Up, up and away	Krill Roslyakov
Page 22	Hand on Bulb	Benjamin Howell
Page 23	Fatal Freedom	Ajmone Tristano
Page 26	Exit stage left	Kimberly Hall
Page 27	Hand authentication	Undergroundarts.co.uk
Page 28	Gearing up	Donald Sawvel
Page 30	Reaction	John Foxx
Page 32	They are watching	sn4ke
Page 33	Emotions	Yannis Ntousiopoulos
Page 36	six speed	Matthew Jacques
Page 37	rust	Stephen Mulcahey
Page 38	missles	Falko Matte
Page 39	World view	Lorelyn Medina
Page 40	Time in pieces	unknown
Page 42	Doorway	Tatiana53
Page 44	The String	ZTS
Page 45	Survivor	David Brimm
Page 46	Full Circle	jgl247
Page 48	Aliens among us	Chris Harvey

VISUAL TRANSLATION

VISUAL TRANSLATION

VISUAL TRANSLATION

FREE BRAIN TUNE-UP

radicalpumpboy.com

The cover of SunBurn has been UV coated for added protection at the beach.